RUNNING DOWN A DREAM

RYAN J. PELTON

THE
PROLIFIC
WRITER PRESS

Printed in the United States of America

First Printing, 2019

ISBN 978-1-949420-13-5 (print)

The Prolific Writer Press

Kansas City, MO

AUTHOR'S NOTE

Hi reader! I write a lot of books, in a variety of genres, and for a variety of audiences. If you'd like to grab more books like this one, or try something new, please consider joining my author newsletter. I'll keep you updated on my latest releases, I give away lots of exclusive goodies reserved only for my VIP's, and much more.

>>>Join Ryan's Newsletter
(ryanjpelton.com)

Now we've got that covered, let's get to the book.

Happy Reading,

Ryan J. Pelton

CHAPTER 1

I hate the word no. Okay, hate is a strong word. I can live with a no when asking for a ninth slice of sausage pizza from Cirevello's. The best pizza in Los Angeles. But getting a no from Larry Nelson is like kissing your sister. Not that I'd know. My younger brother Octavius is not a girl but acts like one when I destroy him at Space Assent, NFL Football, or Renegade. These are video games. We've never kissed, by the way.

Who is Larry Nelson? Glad you asked.

A balding middle-aged man who is my boss at the Swope Park Golf Course. One of the busiest golf courses in California. Mr. Nelson loves to remind us of these facts when he's storming around the Pro Shop telling me to tuck in my shirt. I've been working at Swope the last two summers. I started in the golf cart barn, washing down electric carts. George, the head of the cart barn, said I wasn't cut out for manual labor. I asked for some inside work and was promoted to the golf shop to organize new merchandise and vacuum the floors multiple times a day. Mr. Nelson says we should be able to eat off the floors. He's weird.

I show up on time and work hard, even when it requires a 4 AM open. I even put up with Mr. Walker, an eighty-five-year-old golfer with no ounce of compassion in his frail bones. He once told me his wife could beat me up in a boxing match. Something I'd rather not find out. Getting beat up by an old lady would only add to the perception Mr. Nelson has of me.

So I've been busting my butt for two summers and selective weekends during the school year, between basketball and football season at Carver High School. Neglecting any semblance of a social life and stuffing every penny in my bank account for the goal of all goals. My registration fee for the International Gaming Olympics in Denver.

Since the ripe age of ten, after receiving my first game console, PlayStation 3, I had a path in life. Gaming champ. I'd heard of Jaedong, a master of Starcraft; Jonathan Wendel, a Quake champ; and who could forget: Buster McKenna. The reigning international champ who never loses at any game. I'd take my $3000 of hard earned cash and pay for my registration, lodging, travel, and some extra money for food. I had it all figured out and I could see my name, Darius Montgomery, in lights. Watching the likes of Jaedong, Wendel, and McKenna fall to the ground in defeat. The crowds now chanting my name... Darius... Darius... you're the best! And then a small voice coming from the back of the stadium, the prettiest of all the gamers, Samantha Witherspoon, giving me a kiss on the cheek and asking if I wanted to see a movie.

It was perfect. Win the $50,000 grand prize, help the family, and all would be right in the world. I hadn't slept well, knowing the tournament was right around the corner.

Until some lazy college kid named Rory ruined everything.

Mr. Nelson won't give me the time off from work. I hate no's. He said we're shorthanded because Rory quit. A college kid who can't seem to get out of bed. Larry's words, not mine.

I've been slaving away at the golf course for two summers, saving every penny for this moment. An opportunity to play in the tournament of all tournaments (If you're a gamer). I would've registered last summer but had two problems. One, I didn't have my driver's license yet. And you had to be sixteen to enter. This summer, check and check.

The only other hurdle to qualify for the IGO was to win a regional event. I beat Henry Thompson in a game of Freedom Fighters last month to punch my ticket to the promised land. And Larry Nelson (and Rory), my cranky boss, will destroy my dreams of being the IGO champ.

I hate no's.

"Can you please put away that stupid video game magazine? What a waste of brain cells. We have customers," Larry said, standing with his hands on his hips. A look of, *I think your generation is lazy and have it easy*, on his face.

I closed *Gamer Addict* and tossed it onto the back counter. I then punched my code into the cash register and sighed. I glanced behind me and noticed the golf shop was empty. "Sorry, boss. We had a lull in the action. Thought I'd catch up on some reading. The competition at the International Gaming Olympics looks stiff. Too bad I'll never know if I can hang with the best in the world," I said, with extra snark, hoping it would make Mr. Nelson feel bad.

But Larry Nelson doesn't feel.

Nelson tapped his chubby fingers on the counter and yanked up his khakis, which were falling underneath his sagging midsection. "I told you Darius... we're short handed after Rory quit. I'm sorry your little video game thingy isn't going to happen. Maybe you could use your remaining brain cells on something more productive. Like making Swope Park the best course in LA. "

"Yes, a worthy goal. But can't you find a replacement from Oak Mills? This tournament is kind of a big deal."

Nelson wiped mustard from the corner of his mouth from downing three hotdogs minutes earlier. "You want to be some video game champ. How about a comedian? That's a good joke. I'd never have any of those hacks from Oak Mills work at my course. We run the third busiest course in LA. I will not ruin our reputation with those losers. The last time I used one of their guys they stole money."

"Isn't Oak Mills the second busiest course in California?"

Nelson ignored the comment.

"Come on, Mr. Nelson. I'll work extra shifts for the rest of the summer. I just need a week off. How about you don't pay me an entire week when I get back from the tournament? I'll volunteer my time," I said with a smile, and reached out a hand to Nelson, "Deal?"

He looked at my hand like it was on fire. It was coming. I hated the word. Despised the word. Nelson's stony heart wasn't changing today. I knew it, and everyone else knew it. Larry Nelson never changes his mind.

"No," Nelson said.

Larry Nelson was a middle aged man who served in the Army in the early eighties. He was part of a squad that bombed Beirut and took down Gaddafi. Depending on who you ask, I think Nelson has PTSD. Nelson is on his third marriage and has a hard time letting people get close to him.

Not to be a jerk, but I don't care. He has no right to treat his employees like useless hirelings. I just want the time off for the tournament in Denver, and he's ruining my life. He could find a sub. I know, he's done it before.

And that's why I had to quit.

CHAPTER 2

THE CHAPMAN FLATS APARTMENTS HAVE BEEN HOME since Mom died. Five years ago my mother got cancer in her pancreas. Doctors say it's the worst type to get. Mom was a fighter and held on for a year before she went to heaven. Dad moved the family into The Flats to save money for paying off massive amounts of medical bills. He said we'd move to a better part of town after he got on his feet. We're still trying to find our footing.

My 1995 Honda Civic pulled into a parking spot in front of the apartment. I banged my head on the steering wheel, brainstorming a story for why I quit my job. Except in this movie, I would not say anything about quitting, not yet. Money is tight, like always, and it would break Dad's heart knowing I quit a decent paying job without talking with him. I've been pitching in some extra cash from tips at the golf course. Dad says every penny helps. I slammed the door and played a few versions of my story in my head.

Marcus Thigpen waved from his balcony on the second floor as I neared our front door. He sat in a wheelchair stroking a white cat and smoking a cigarette. Marcus had been in the "hood" for the last thirty years. He said he'd love to get out to another part of town but the liability checks wouldn't cut it for a move. Normal for our area. Everyone dreams of greener grass on the other side of town, but reality bites. I unlocked the door of our apartment and told Marcus to have a good night.

Before I crossed the threshold Octavius punched me in the stomach.

"What the heck dude?" I said, rubbing my stomach. My backpack fell to the ground.

"Opened a new level on Star Games."

"Good for you, loser. Did you need to punch me?"

"Yes, that's what annoying little brothers do."

"Go back to your game, I need to talk to Dad. I'll show you how to play Star Games when I get back from chatting with Dad."

Octavius stuck out his tongue. "I'm not scared of you. But be careful, Dad isn't in a good mood."

"What happened?"

"Ask him yourself."

Michael Montgomery, or Mikey, is a prideful man. Never admits defeat and has a hard time asking for help. Will do anything to take care of his family. He would make a good gamer, but thinks it's a waste of time. He slumped at the dining room table in the kitchen and nursed a coffee. He glanced at me. "How was work, kid? Any tips?"

"Uh, good, I think. Sometimes shifts go by so fast you're not sure where the time goes. I made a couple extra bucks. Mr. Kim said to put it toward the college fund," I said, slamming a twenty on the kitchen table. Dad didn't flinch and swiped the bill and crammed it into his jean pocket.

"Every penny helps... Where does the time go? Feels like yesterday I was marrying your mom and having you little brats," he said, sipping on the coffee from a World's Best Dad mug.

I smiled and played the script in my head. "Uh, well, yeah, so how was your day? Anything exciting happening at the shop?"

"Not my best day. Willy smashed a tow truck into a fire hydrant and got fired."

"Willy Loman? The guy with the gold tooth? Oh man, that's big. You okay? Seem upset over it."

Dad gripped the coffee mug with both hands and finished the last bit of black liquid. "I got fired, too. The owner, Rick, said if I hadn't hired Willy the company wouldn't have to shovel out a bunch of cash for the damages. Somehow I got blamed for it. I think Rick is a racist," Dad said, mumbling under his breath.

"That's not fair. You're the best employee at Roger's Towing. They'd be out of business without you running things. Is Rick a racist?"

"I'm sorry, kid. I've let you and Octavius down. Ever since Mom died, I can't seem to catch a break. Back to the drawing board, I guess," Dad said, staring off in the distance.

Dad worked three jobs when Mom was going through chemo treatments. Insurance only covered a portion of the bills. He even delivered pizzas for the Pizza Shack at night to keep the lights on. When he got a midnight shift as a dispatcher for Roger's Towing, they later hired him to run the shop. I'm not sure Dad slept for the year Mom was in the hospital.

I reached out a hand and placed it on Dad's. It was rough, like he'd lived three lifetimes. "You'll find another job. You always do."

He sighed. "I wish we could move out of this hole. The

garbage disposal is broken again, and the sink is leaking. The super never comes over to fix it. I guess you get what you pay for. At least you have your job. Maybe you could pick up some extra shifts while I look for work?"

The defeat in Dad's voice was palpable. How in the world was I going to tell him I quit my job today? The timing couldn't be any worse. I tried to change the subject. "Did the mail come today?"

Dad nodded toward a pile of envelopes sitting on a small table near the front door. I scampered to the table and thought of Plan B. A thick envelope with an orange stamp caught my eye. "No way! It's here." I ripped open the envelope and read the letter.

I let the moment sink in. "I got in the tournament..."

Dad shrugged and did not understand what I meant. Octavius tossed off his gaming headset and ran over to the table. "You did it, big bro. How you getting to the tourney?"

"Well, I'm going to take a week off from work. I'll drive to Denver in a day, play the tournament, and drive back. Since I'll win the International Gaming Olympics, seven days will be the perfect amount of time."

I feared turning around because everything sounded perfect in my head. Except one minor detail. I never told Dad I had registered for the IGO. He didn't even know I'd won the regional event a few weeks back. Dad was not against gaming, in principle. He bought us our gaming systems, and would scrape up some cash for a new game, once in a while. But he wanted to make sure we worked hard in school and got good jobs. He knew the stress of struggling financially and sometimes life throws you curveballs, in the form of cancer. Do the responsible thing, he'd say. Gaming for a career was not the stability he'd hoped for for his son.

Dad slid away from the kitchen table and casually walked over to our conversation. "What are you boys talking about?" he asked in a hushed tone.

Octavius said, "Darius got into the biggest gaming tournament in the world. He's driving to Denver to play. How cool is that?"

I slapped Octavius on the arm. He'd blown my cover and the moment couldn't be worse for breaking the news to Dad about the tournament. Oh yeah, not to mention I quit my job. "Is this true, Darius Jamal Montgomery?"

Not good, the full name. When the full name comes out, Dad ain't happy.

"Well, you see. I was going to tell you sooner but kind of forgot. Things have been crazy with work, school, you know... life stuff."

Dad didn't have to say a word. He wanted the truth and wanted it now.

"Here's the deal. I played in a local gaming tournament down at the Staples Center. I thought it would be fun to see if I could get into the International Gaming Olympics. You had to win the whole thing to get into the tourney in Denver. Well, I won, and like they say, the rest is history. I was going to tell you, I promise."

"What about work? You can't take a week off and drive to Denver. They need you at the course. And we need the money."

"Mr. Nelson gave me the time off. Not a problem. One week and I'll come right back. If I win the tournament, I get $50,000. Imagine what we could do with that kind of money. We could get out of here for sure."

Dad brushed the side of his face. His eyebrows narrowed in. He moved in close and tapped my chest. "You think winning some stupid video game tournament is the answer to our problems? No amount of money will bring Mom back. You understand?"

"Dad, I didn't say that. I just want to help."

"You can help by going to school, staying out of trouble, and working your job. I'll worry about the money stuff."

Octavius glanced at me and wondered what I was going to say next. We could feel the chill and tension in the air of our small apartment.

"Dad, come on. It's only a week. I'm doing good in school. I want to play in the tournament. It means a lot to me. I think I can win."

Dad backed away and smiled. But this smile wasn't a friendly one, it had a menace to it.

"We all lost when Mom died. Deal with it. Don't even think of going to that stupid tournament. I'm going to bed."

CHAPTER 3

I'D DESTROYED OCTAVIUS IN STAR GAMES THE NIGHT before. He talked trash about finding new levels but hadn't run into the master gamer, Darius Montgomery. No way my kid brother will ever beat the future IGO champion. But I'll say, the late night gaming session didn't bode well for my first period chemistry class. Not to mention I tossed and turned all night, my mind racing from the altercation with Dad. I hated disappointing my father, and he still doesn't know I quit my job at the golf course. So there's that.

"Mr. Montgomery. Care to tell me what the letter H represents on the periodic table?"

The class giggled as I nodded off and banged my head on my desk.

I raised my head from the desk, wiped some drool from my mouth, and could feel the eyes of the classroom bearing down on me. My mind was foggy and the sharp preceptors of numbers and words and data failed me. "Why don't you call on someone else? It wouldn't be fair to deprive the future leaders of our country the opportunity to learn. I'll save my chemistry knowledge for another time."

The class gave out a low rumble of laughter. Mrs. Reed didn't find my response amusing. "Chemistry knowledge, huh? Glad to see your sense of humor is working between naps. Maybe more time on the books and less time on video games, Mr. Montgomery. Since you are a future leader of this country," Mrs. Reed said, jutting out a hip and giving a smile.

"Seems to be the theme of my life right now."

"Excuse me, Mr. Montgomery. Did you say something? Something you want to share with the entire class?"

"No, ma'am. You just sound a lot like my dad."

I mimicked holding a video game controller. "But you should see me in action, Mrs. Reed. I'm fantastic at video games. I just need to figure out how to leverage it for a career."

Reed shook her head and moved toward the whiteboard in the front of the classroom. "More books... fewer games..."

I yelled out, "Hydrogen. The H on the periodic table is Hydrogen."

Mrs. Reed turned back, gave a smile, and called on another student.

Then the bell rang.

We piled out of class for lunch. I found Edgar Swamp. My best friend. We met at Booker T. Washington Middle School when I moved into The Flats. I had gone to the same school for all of elementary and moving to a new school wasn't easy for an awkward middle schooler. We play basketball together on the high school team and bond over hours and hours of video games. Edgar isn't as passionate about gaming as me, but we always have a good time.

"You all right, Darius? Your face says either girl troubles, or late night gaming session."

"Are those the same faces?"

"At times. Your skills with video games are far superior than with the ladies. If you spent less time honing your gaming skills and a little more on asking a girl on a date, you might not spend the summer alone."

"I have a lot going on right now. If you want to be the best gamer in the world, the social life will take a hit. Girls can wait."

"I know you're the big gamer hotshot. It's okay to take a break from Star Wars and beating your latest high score to have a pizza with someone from the opposite sex."

"It's not Star Wars. Star Games, lame-o."

"Thanks for the correction... gaming nerd. So what's *really* going on?"

"Not much. I quit my job. Told my dad I was going to Denver to play in the International Gaming Olympics. He said no. My life is pretty much over. That's all..."

"Wait, what? You quit your job? Why did you do that? Don't you need to help with the family bills?"

"Not my best moment in sixteen years of life."

"Why did you quit? Mr. Nelson finally break you?"

"Remember when I played in the gaming regional event at Staples Center? Well, I won, and got invited to play in the IGO. Nelson wouldn't give me the time off, so I quit."

"Dang, man, just like that. That took balls. Does your dad know?"

"He knows about the tournament. Didn't even flinch when he said I can't go. Not the job. Oh yeah, and to make things more sucky. Dad lost his job at the towing company. So nobody be paying bills right now."

"Wasn't he running things over there?"

"Pretty much. He thinks it was racism. The owner never liked him."

"You don't always have to play the race card. We're

minorities living in a hostile world, but I'm sure there's more to it. He'll find more work somewhere. He always does."

"Sure. But right now nobody has a job. I want to play in the biggest gaming tournament in the world, and everyone seems to think it's a bad idea. When do you just take a leap of faith and see where the pixels fall? What do you think?"

Edgar sipped on a Mountain Dew. "Pixels? You wonder why you have no dates. If it were me. I'd go. Just go... What's the worst that can happen? It's the last week of school. Summer break is essentially already in session. We're going to be seniors next year. Let's make this summer an unforgettable one. One we can tell our grandkids about. You only live once, kid."

I hesitated while ripping into a piece of pepperoni pizza. "I don't know. We could lose our apartment. My dad could kill me. Should I go on?"

Edgar waved it off. "We only have today. Let the pixels fall, or whatever you said."

I wiped my fingers of grease from the cafeteria pizza. "Wait, what's all this 'we' talk? You want to go to Denver with me?"

"Yeah, man. I'm your wingman and best friend. You can't road trip without your support system in place. It's one week. This is your dream, you have to ignore the naysayers."

"What will you tell your parents?"

"I don't know. Something about supporting the greatest gamer of all time. Or witnessing history in the making."

"I'd keep brainstorming. Your folks already hate when we play games deep into the night. Say we're killing brain cells."

"It's fine. I'll make something up. Tell them I'm going to visit my uncle in Phoenix for a week. It'll work out. A summer to never forget," Edgar, said, reaching for a high five.

I sat at the lunchroom table and scanned the room. I watched kids of all shapes and sizes conversing at tables. Some sitting alone, some throwing food, and others laughing with soda shooting out of their noses. I wondered what the point of high school was? Why spend so much effort doing things that don't mean all that much. I had a dream, why couldn't I pursue it? Edgar was right. No one could stop me. *You only live once.*

CHAPTER 4

WHEN YOU'RE DEVISING A PLAN TO DRIVE CROSS country without your dad knowing, it helps to have a job at a golf course. The worst part of the job are the early mornings. I have to open the shop by 4 AM to let the golf cart barn guys in, allow the greens keepers to water, and get the course ready for play. And I have to go through all my tee times to make sure everyone gets out on time. A perfect cover for avoiding the wrath of Dad for a few days.

The bad part of working at a golf course... is I no longer work at a golf course. A little lie for your dreams to come true. That's okay, right? You'd do it. I'll tell Dad the truth at some point. I'm not a monster. A simple story: I'll be working opening and closing at the course and then spending the night at Edgar's. I'll then open again the next day, another night at Edgar's. I'm thinking a couple days of this and Dad won't get suspicious. Octavius will cover if he suspects anything. That's all I have for now. I'll figure out the rest on the road. I can at least get to Denver and win the tournament. When I'm the International Gaming Champ, Dad won't care I told a little lie, right?

Edgar sat in the front seat of the Civic and opened a cooler between his legs. "Mountain Dew, check. Red Bull, check. Cell phone chargers, check, copies of Gamer Addict, check," he then reached into his backpack, "Candy bars and Doritos, check. If we need anything else, we can get it on the road. We're doing it, man. We're really doing it. You only live once..."

I watched the joy on Edgar's face and couldn't shake my tension of excitement and anxiety. Playing in the biggest gaming tournament in the world was everything I'd dreamed of since my first gaming console at age ten. But also a low hum anxiety for lying to Dad, a worry about money after Dad losing his job (and me quitting mine), and what if I don't have the game to compete with the best in the world?

I popped open a Dew and slammed down half a can. "Is this a good idea?"

Edgar opened a Dew, too. "Drinking Mountain Dew at four in the morning is not recommended by most pediatricians."

"No, stupid. All of it. Are we dumb to think this is a good idea, on any level?"

"Darius... my man. Let's get honest. You were doing this whether I said anything or not. I know you. You just needed a little nudge. How your dad responds is another story."

I placed the can of soda in the cup holder and slapped Edgar on the side of his Los Angeles Lakers hat. "Seriously? That's not what I needed right now. Dad will come around when I'm champ. You'll see."

Edgar nodded and sipped on the Dew. "Anything we forgot?"

I pulled out into the dark streets of LA. "I'm sure if we forgot anything important we can pick it up on the road.

Remember, between the two of us, money is tight. I'm spending every dollar I have on earth for this tournament. Money for gas, snacks, drinks, and not much else. I have to save everything for the lodging and some other fees at the tournament. You're chipping in for gas money, too. Don't rip me off like when we went to the Foo Fighters concert. Remember, I paid for your hotdog and Coke and it cost like twenty-three dollars. You said you'd pay me the following week. Well, that was last summer."

Edgar raised his hands. "I'm good for it. Here..." he opened a leather wallet and tossed a twenty at me, "I'll get you the three later."

"Where'd you get money? You're always mooching off me."

"The lawn business is going well. Not many customers in the hood, but the rich folks in Brentwood and Bel Air are putting some nice change in my pocket."

"Look at you, little entrepreneur. So why are you always asking me for money?"

"They say the rich never spend their own money. They use other peoples money. Think of yourself as my investor."

"You're an idiot. Plan on filling up the tank next stop. Money bags."

Edgar glanced into the backseat as we made our way to the highway. "What's that black blanket in the backseat about? Is your suitcase under there?"

I turned my head as I hit the blinker to ease onto the highway. "That's weird. Our suitcases are in the trunk. I don't remember putting anything under the blanket in the back. I guess it's early, anything is possible."

As I pulled onto the on-ramp of the 405 a car swerved into my lane. I slammed on the brakes to let him pull out in front. The candy bars and chips slid on the floor and Edgar slammed into the dashboard. "Easy, kid. Learn how to drive," Edgar said, rubbing his chest.

"Sorry, man. That jerk cut me off. Did you hear something from the back seat?"

"Probably my fart from your terrible driving. I pass gas when I'm nervous."

"You must be nervous a lot."

"Funny guy. Pay attention to the road. And get us to Colorado in one piece."

I scratched my head. "Are you sure you heard nothing from the back seat? I thought I heard a moan."

"I'll check." Edgar slammed his hand down on the black blanket in the backseat.

The lump moaned.

CHAPTER 5

Octavius leaned on the back of our seats and smiled in the rear-view mirror. Like one of those 'I'm your little brother and I exist to ruin your life' smiles. He then waved to add insult to injury. "How's it going, big bro? I was hoping to stay in stealth mode until Utah. Surprise!"

I glanced in the mirror and tried to not lose my cool. "I know it's early, so I'm going to chalk it up to hallucinations. No way you'd be stupid enough to pull a stunt like this."

Octavius ruffled his Nirvana tee shirt and adjusted his black skull cap. "Nope. All me. 100% Octavius. Surprised?"

"I wouldn't be more surprised if I woke up with a tail growing out of my backside. Please tell me you have a good explanation for blowing our plans."

"Well, big bro. I liked the original plan of staying behind to hold down the fort. You know, make sure Dad didn't sniff out your shenanigans. But I couldn't let you go halfway across the United States alone with Edgar. He's not the most responsible person. I'm blood, and blood has to stick together. Besides, you'd miss me being gone for a week."

Edgar popped into the conversation. "Easy, little dude.

I'm responsible. The other day a dog with only three legs hobbled into the neighborhood. I called Animal Control. How about that for responsible?" Edgar said, jutting out his slim chest.

Octavius hesitated for a moment. "The same guy who broke up with a girl because she didn't like the Avengers movies? Helping a stray dog doesn't make you responsible."

"If a girl can't get on board with the Marvel Universe, there's no future. Forget about ever being the future Mrs. Swamp. I have to draw the line somewhere."

I said, "Please stop arguing like little old ladies. You're giving me a headache. The bigger issue is the plan. The moment Dad realizes you're gone, we're busted. He will get suspicious."

Octavius shook his head. "Come on, Big Bro. O ye of little faith. I took care of it. Dad won't suspect a thing."

"What did you tell him?"

"I didn't have to tell him anything. It was like the stars aligned and God himself carved a straight path for our journey to Denver. Turns out church camp fell on this very week. I told him I'd be staying at Reggie's house and heading to camp with his folks. Dad bought it, problem solved."

Octavius reached for a high five from the backseat. I ignored the gesture.

"Now I don't feel so bad. Lying about church camp is a new low, even for you. What are you going to tell Dad when camp is done at the end of the week?" I asked.

"I'll think of something. I'm a master liar."

"Probably not something to boast about."

Octavius was a lot of things. But he was a loyal brother. He wanted me to succeed and always had my back. He's known since we were little guys, learning how to game, how bad I want to win the IGO. Everything in my bones wanted to turn the car around and bring Octavius home. Yet something held me back. Maybe the support of little bro meant more than I had realized. Even worth Dad finding out the plan to road trip across the country.

"Here's the deal, little bro. You do as we say, no funny games, or you're on the first bus back to LA. And I hope you brought some money. We're on a tight budget. I can't afford to feed your bottomless stomach."

Octavius yanked out a wallet and held up a wad of cash. "My cash for church camp. I don't need your handouts."

"You're so going to hell," Edgar said.

"I'm serious, or your hitchhiking back. We have about sixteen hours to Denver, if we make minimal stops. So hold your pee and don't drink no Super Big Gulps. You got it, guys?"

"Yes, sir," Octavius said, and saluted.

＝

We drove four hours and made it outside Las Vegas, to a small town called Carson. The drive was quiet, as Edgar and Octavius slept like babies most of the way from the early start. I pulled into a gas station as the sun was in full bloom. I needed to fill up on gas and take a leak.

The Quick Fill looked like something from a horror movie. A plain white building with rotting wood, two gas pumps, and cracked asphalt in the parking lot. Weeds pushed through the cement to top off the creepy exterior. The weather was warm, but not terrible for the desert.

I opened the dirty glass door and heard a bell chime. A deep baritone voice greeted me. "Where you headed, young pup?" An older man wearing coveralls and sipping on a Coke reclined behind the counter.

The deep voice startled me. "Sorry, didn't see you there. Denver."

"Beautiful this time of year. Not too hot, yet. Snow is melted. I could tell you're not from around here."

"That obvious?"

"Ha, not really. People come through here from all over the country. Not much around these parts. Your plates gave you away. California's a nice place. Lived there for a second in the service. San Diego."

"San Diego has perfect weather. I'd do anything to live there. But we don't have that kind of cash."

"You pay for the weather in California."

"True. It's not all bad. I could get used to the open spaces out here. LA's too busy. I've dreamed about a little house in the woods, where I could play video games and not have to deal with people."

"Video games? That doesn't sound all that great. You gotta get out in it. Why not enjoy the stuff God made? Like trees, flowers, and the warm desert air?"

"God made video games, too, right?"

"I guess so. Where are you going? I see you have some sleepy passengers for your travels," the old man said, glancing out the dirty window toward the gas pumps.

I turned and smiled. "Yeah, those are my copilots. My brother and best friend. Headed to a gaming tournament. Not to brag... but I'm one of the best in the country," I said.

"So that's why you'd rather be with your games and not people. Makes sense. I don't understand youth today. They seem to care more about their little devices than being in God's creation. If you don't mind me asking... What's a gaming tournament?"

"Take the best video gamers in the world and put them in one room. Let them battle it out until one of them wins the $50,000 grand prize. There's more to it, but you get the gist."

"Heaven help us! The winner makes that kind of cash? Who knew you could make money playing games. I've always thought you got paid for honest work. I'm in the wrong business, son."

"There are probably better ways to make money. But my minimum wage job at the golf course isn't cutting it. We kind of need the money, too."

The old man glanced out to the Civic. "It appears you're doing okay. You got a car. Traveling across the country with your buddies. Opportunity to play in a tournament. How bad can it be?"

"I guess you're right. We're not starving or anything. My dad lost his job. And my mom got cancer and died. The medical bills stacked up high. I'm just trying to help. Every little bit helps, right? That's what my dad says, at least."

"Sorry to hear that young man. It's a noble thing to help your family like this. $50,000 is a lot of scratch. I'm sure it will help. Help a lot."

"Scratch?" I asked.

"Money. But remember one thing, kid. Money can't buy you happiness. You remind me of myself a long time ago."

"What do you mean?"

The old man asked if I had a couple minutes to see something. I felt a little uncomfortable, not knowing the man for more than five minutes. But I obliged, and he led me to the back of the gas station. A small shack with a rickety screen door was attached to the station.

He led me inside.

The walls were filled with pictures. It looked like the

shack hadn't been cleaned in years. A small stove and kitchen table sat in the middle of the space. A bed was in the corner, with covers strewn on the floor. "You live here?"

"Home, sweet home. All them pictures are my family. I call that wall my Happy Place."

I strolled the small space and looked at the pictures. "They still around?"

"Most of them."

"They live out here?"

"Yes, sir. We have lunch every Sunday. Most of them live within an hour of here. We're not a perfect family, but we sure love each other."

"Sounds cool. I bet you wish you could live somewhere else. You know, a place with cable and the internet. Maybe a bigger place?"

"How do you know I haven't had those things? Remember when I said I was like you. All true. I used to live in Las Vegas with my wife. We both were realtors and croupiers on the weekends."

"Croupiers?"

"Dealers at the casinos in Vegas. It was a great life for a time. We made tons of money, had a big house, and all the toys you could imagine. Even had cable," the man said, and smiled, "Then it all ended."

"What happened?"

"My wife got sick. A disease doctors said you'd only see once in your career. She died, and I moved back here."

"Yeah, death sucks. Why did you move out here?"

"It's my home. Where my family have spent most of their lives. My great-great grandparents moved from Ireland to find a better life here in Nevada. We haven't always had much money, but we've made it work. Joy doesn't come from having a lot of stuff. We have each other and that seems to be enough."

I couldn't believe what I was hearing. I complain when the internet is down, or the traffic is bad on the 405. This guy has nothing, and he's the happiest dude I've ever met. But one thing was certain, winning the tournament and getting $50,000 was going to change my family's future.

The old man ushered me out the door. "Thanks for taking a stroll down memory lane with me. I hope you find what you're looking for at the tournament, kid."

I thanked him for his time, took a leak, and filled up the car with gas. Octavius woke up and wiped crust from his eye. "Where are we?"

"Nevada, outside Las Vegas. You guys haven't made a sound since we left LA. I'm not going to lie. It was kind of nice."

I turned on the car and gently eased my way out of the gas station. Edgar woke up and glanced into the side mirror. The old man was waving from the front of the gas station. "Who's the old guy?"

"I made a new friend. Man, sometimes old dudes drop some serious truth bombs."

Octavius asked, "What did he say?"

"Talked about where true happiness comes from."

"Mountain Dew and video games?"

"No, dork. We talked about some deep stuff. He showed me his place."

"He lives in the gas station?"

"Sort of. He lives behind the station, in a little room. Seemed like a real and genuine guy. Kind of keeping things in check for me."

"You nervous about the tournament?"

"While you guys were sleeping, I was doing a lot of

thinking. I'm not sure this is a good idea. I lied to Dad, and it's weighing on me. Octavius lied, and I feel responsible. What kind of role model am I?"

Octavius reached into his jeans pocket and pulled out a necklace with a cross dangling from the bottom. "You're a great role model, big bro. I can make my own choices."

I nodded and appreciated his comment.

"I wanted to find a good time to give you this. Mom gave it to me and said it gave her strength during her cancer treatments. She got it as a little girl. Her dad gave it to her, and she always believed the symbol of the cross had a mysterious power. I want you to have it. When you want to give up, sometimes you need to look outside yourself."

"Dang, bro. That was deep. I don't know what to say."

"Nothing, let's not make this awkward. Just wear the cross. Hope it helps. And don't worry about me, I'm a big boy and can handle whatever consequences come from Dad and our little adventure. I'm just glad to be with you, guy."

Edgar said, "Okay, let's stop. We don't need to have a cry fest. Remember, we're dudes."

I put on the cross and thought about my mom. She was such a giving person and the glue of our family. Then my mind drifted to the old man and what he'd said about happiness. I wish all of it gave me a new confidence. But the low hum of anxiety and worry came full force.

I'd hoped more of the open road would settle my nerves. Only time would tell.

CHAPTER 6

The drive from Las Vegas to Albuquerque would take eight hours with no stops. With the small bladders of Octavius and Edgar there was no way we'd make that kind of time. I rolled down the window of the Civic and let the warm breezes of the desert splash my face. I felt sleepy, but the adrenaline of the adventure kept me alert on the open road.

My mind drifted off to Dad, and I wondered how the job search was going. Wondered if he had suspicions I was not at work and was driving across the country to find me. Parents have this sixth sense when their kids are up to something. I couldn't dwell on it too long or my stomach hurt. Edgar and Octavius linked their DS devices and played Mario Brothers in the back seat. They were surprisingly easy riding companions.

Oh yeah, so why New Mexico? A quick travel trip, if you're going from LA to Denver, going through New Mexico in the Southwest direction isn't the fastest route. You go through Utah. Okay, you're welcome for the geography lesson.

Two more reasons. I love the show Breaking Bad and they shot it in Albuquerque. I was hoping to get a glimpse of the house Walter White lived in and some other landmarks of the iconic TV show. Edgar is a big fan, too, so we had to do it. We'd bonded many nights binging it on Netflix after basketball games.

Second, Buster McKenna. Who is Buster? Glad you asked. The reigning international gaming champ. I ran into Buster online when playing a game of Quake. Let's say he kicked my butt all over the interwebs, and it wasn't even close. In a moment of delusion I could hang with him, but it was clear he's a champ for a reason. I lay awake at night dreaming about beating Buster.

My gaming skills are solid. But when I played Buster it was like a one-year-old learning to walk. Awkward, wobbly, and a lot of crying. Quake isn't my best game but I should've had a better showing if I'm going to take him down at the IGO. Oh yeah, Buster lives in the hometown of Walter White. I'm not sure why I'm curious where Buster lives in New Mexico. Hoping some of his gaming magic will rub off on me? Who knows?

Edgar took off his earbuds. "We to Albuquerque yet? I want to see Walter White's house."

"Not even close. We're still in Arizona. A few more hours. How's little bro doing against you in Mario Bros.?"

Edgar smirked. "He's getting dominated. You mess with the best, you die like the rest."

I smirked. "Whatever. Your skills aren't nice. I'm the one heading to the IGO. Besides, I hate those handheld games. They're for little kids, not serious gamers. Come play Halo and we'll see who's standing."

"Don't think too highly of yourself. The Apostle Paul said that," said Edgar.

"Okay, preacher man. I'll try to keep that in mind. Come on, Octo-Man, don't let Edgar beat you. You're making the family look bad," I said, glancing out into the vast desert sky.

Octavius removed one ear bud. "Look bad? How about when Buster McKenna destroyed you online? You have no chance against that guy. Why are you driving by his house? You have a crush on him?"

"No, I don't have a man crush on Buster. I have a thing for New Mexico. It's an enchanted place."

"How would you know? You've never been out of the hood."

"The internet. And Breaking Bad. The desert has a magical quality to it. You know what I mean?"

"Whatever."

"And thanks for supporting my dreams, little bro. I can beat Buster, I just need another shot. Too many mental mistakes. It was right after prom and I was tired."

"No excuses. Pro gamers don't make excuses."

"Truth. Just give me another shot. That's all I can ask for. I've been training and I'm ready."

"Chugging Mountain Dew and eating Doritos is hardly training."

I reached to the backseat and gave Edgar a fist bump. "Gamer life, yo."

"You guys are lame," Octavius said, glancing out of the window, "What's so great about the desert? How many bodies they must bury out in those open spaces must be off the charts."

"You have a dark imagination. When you live in a busy city your entire life there's always something cool about the country and open spaces. Easier to breathe in the fresh air. Remember when Dad and Mom took us to Palm Desert for vacations? We'd get those cheap motel rooms in the middle of summer because it was hotter than the sun. We'd swim all day, and you'd always get ear infections. Those were good memories."

"Yeah, how could I forget? You used to drown me in the deep end before I could swim."

"You still can't swim."

"I have PTSD from those vacations in the desert. I blame you for my lack of swimming skills."

"You're just uncoordinated."

We bantered and laughed our way through the Arizona and New Mexico desert for the next six hours. It had been a while since my mind was free of the anxieties and worries of school, jobs, and money. Maybe the desert was just the enchanted place I needed to prepare for winning the tournament.

We pulled into New Mexico around early afternoon. I veered the Civic onto a quiet street and parked in front of ranch-style house with white stucco and brown trim. The Walter White House. It was located in an area of Albuquerque called Northeastern Heights. We smashed our faces against the windows and thought about Breaking Bad. At least Edgar and I did, Octavius could not care less.

"This is a waste of time. Did we really add time to our trip to Denver to see a fictional house from TV?" Octavius said, slumping in the backseat.

Edgar placed a finger over his lips. "Never speak ill of the greatest TV show of all time. This means a lot to us. Give us our moment."

I said in a hushed tone, "What do you think it was like filming Breaking Bad? You think Bryan Cranston is a cool dude in real life?"

"He's got to be. I saw him on Jimmy Kimmel once. He seemed like an authentic dude."

Octavius stuck a finger in his mouth and pretended to gag. "Can you stop the man crushes and move on. Forget Buster McKenna, Darius, you have a crush on Walter White. Let's get some food and play video games."

"One second," I said, hopping out of the Civic, and walking up the driveway. Edgar leaned out of the passenger window and whispered, "Dude, you can't just trespass on a stranger's property. You'd get shot in the hood."

I held up a hand and told them to give me a second. I snapped a picture of the driveway and front of the house. A man opened the door and yelled, "Get out of here, tourists."

I jetted back to the Civic and peeled out to find some food and video games before Octavius became cranky.

We found a place called Twister's. The restaurant used for the Los Pollos Hermanos episodes in Breaking Bad. Except they didn't serve chicken, only hotdogs and burgers.

Edgar and I pretended it was chicken, like the show.

CHAPTER 7

As we drove into late afternoon, weariness from the trip set in. The food from Twister's was fantastic but I might've overdone it with an extra chili dog and too much orange soda. We all had soda hangovers, and it wasn't helping keep my eyes open.

Call it an obsession or a man-crush. Regardless, I wanted to see the places Buster McKenna hung out. He was a mythical creature in the gaming world. With a little social media stalking, I'd nailed down an arcade Buster hung out at from time to time. Geekon was a vintage video game arcade and restaurant. The days of legit video game arcades were things of the past. Gone with the dinosaurs. Just like the malls they often belonged to. Smart entrepreneurs were rehabbing some games our parents and the generation before used to play. Donkey Kong, Space Invaders, Pac-Man, and other newer titles like Street Fighter, NBA Jam, and Mortal Kombat.

Money was tight, thankfully we only had to pay $5 each for unlimited games. Not to mention all the water and chips and salsa you could eat. A kid's heaven. Not so much for the waiters. I wondered if we'd run into Buster. A shot in the dark, yes. But I wanted to snoop around and see if I could gain insight and wisdom for why Buster is such a legit gamer. Was there something he had that others didn't? I would find out.

I ordered a water, and the waitress stared me down. Three dudes with no money was food services worst enemy. No food or drinks equals no tips. I get it. It's tough out there. I lived off tips from the golf course. My hourly wage enough to put gas in the car and little else. Tips were my lifeline. An old man gave me a hundred dollar tip for no other reason than having a good day at the course. Score, Darius.

Octavius challenged Edgar to a game of Mortal Kombat. He made quick work of him. I guess Octo-man was right. The handheld games were not his thing. But he had a good strategy and touch with the old school games like MK. Octavius even knew most of the fatal moves. It would make kids from the 80s and 90s proud. Edgar was not much of a gamer and played for the social aspects. Just to be with the guys. Everyone has their reasons.

I later played NBA Jam with Edgar. Showed him up with an old school Cleveland Cavaliers team of Mark Price and Brad Daugherty. "You're cheating. Every time I try to dunk, you foul me," Edgar yelled out, elbowing me in the ribs.

"Yeah, that's kind of the point of the game. No fouls. Playground ball. Don't be jealous of my sweet dunks. Just like real basketball."

Edgar was tired of my trash talking and stormed off to find a bathroom.

I found a table and finished a bowl of chips and salsa. Kids of all ages were playing games. Dads with daughters and sons with mothers. Nothing like seeing families bond over arcade games. People say gaming is a waste of time. Adding to the violence of the culture. Possibly a thread of truth to these claims. Who knows?

My best memories of growing up are playing games with my brother and friends and my mom, when she was alive. Even Dad, occasionally. He never liked video games but would give a football game a chance once in a while. He played guard at East Los Angeles High School and had some college scouts take an interest. Dad had other interests, like meeting my mom and having a kid, or two (me and my brother). He needed to find a job to make ends meet.

Despite not loving video games, Dad tries. He constantly asks what buttons do what and throws the controller when I score all over him in football. When my mom was dying of cancer and wasn't able to do much, we found solace in gaming. Gaming was a hideaway for a brief moment, to forget the pain of life. It didn't heal us or save us like our pastor talks about. But it helped, I can't explain it. It bonded us. Gaming had some magic hard to describe.

I sipped the water and called the waitress over for more chips and salsa. She rolled her eyes and snatched the empty basket away. It's hard out there, I get it.

Octavius give a fist pump after defeating a level on Street Fighter. He beat Zangief, a large Russian fighter, which isn't an easy out.

Then it happened.

I couldn't believe what my young eyes were seeing. Buster McKenna, in all his glory, waltzed into Geekon. He stood about six foot four, chubby, with a flattop. Not the cool gamer vibe I'd expected from someone who took down Dae Jong with ease in last year's Olympics. I'd seen pictures of Buster online but they aren't always accurate. I imaged a suave kid, with black hair slicked to the side. Designer jeans and girls hanging off his arms. Paparazzi snapping pictures for good measure. Buster was ordinary. It lessened the anxiety of losing just because of his looks. It's superficial, but what do you want from me, I'm a teenager? I had to say something to Buster. I blurted out the first thing to come to mind. "Hey, McKenna. You want to play Mortal Kombat?"

The entire arcade glanced in my direction as I held my water. I guess Buster was a big deal in these parts of New Mexico, as others had already stopped what they were doing to stare at the champ. I now regretted opening my big mouth. Edgar and Octavius saw me place a foot in my mouth and came running to my side. "Who's the ogre?" Edgar whispered.

"My nemesis."

"That Buster dude? What's with the flattop? Is he in the Marines?"

"I know, right? Bart Simpson called and wants his hair back," I said, taking a huge gulp of water and sliding the cup across the table. "That's right, Buster. You, me, and Mortal Kombat. Think you can handle it? Or are you chicken?"

Octavius leaned in and whispered in my ear. "Okay, Biff, you can tone down the Back to the Future lines."

"Sorry, I'm nervous. I quote movies when I'm nervous."

Buster strolled over in our direction with two smaller friends walking on each side. One kid had a baseball cap turned backward and wore baggy jeans. He had a lot of freckles. The other kid was almost as tall as Buster and wore a Sacramento Kings jersey. He had braces and a round face.

The kid with the hat spoke up. "Buster doesn't have time for losers like you. He's in training for a tournament starting this week. Please go away."

Octavius came up from behind me and peered around

my body. He gave Buster a look up and down. He whispered to me, "Darius, he's a monster. He could eat you for lunch. No, seriously, I think he must eat people."

"Okay, little bro. Calm down. I'm not asking to fight him. Just play a video game."

"Yeah, but if he decides he doesn't like you he will eat you. And then eat me and Edgar. I'm sure of it. I'm not going out like that."

"Shut up before you get all of us killed."

I cleared my throat and tried to stand tall. Foolproof strategy for intimidating a giant. "You and me, best of five. Mortal Kombat. Call it a warmup for the tournament."

The two kids next to Buster sneered. The kid in the Kings jersey said, "Buster doesn't have time for trash like you. He only plays true gamers."

"Trash like me? True gamers? I know your type. The little guys that hang around real winners to feel better about themselves. That's why these losers hang around me," I said, glancing at Octavius and Edgar standing to the side.

Edgar said, "Easy, dude."

Buster pushed the kids at his sides out of the way and stood a few feet from my face. "You think I need these guys doing my dirty work? I eat bigger plates of food than you for breakfast. I ain't scared of no city kid."

"How do you know I'm a city kid?"

"You have a look."

"What does a city kid look like?"

"Saggy pants, a Foo Fighters tee shirt. Kids dressed like you."

"Okay, well, I can tell you're not a city kid. You have a smell."

"What's that?"

"Nothing."

"Enough, city boy. Let's play."

"Let's do it, then. Best of five. A warmup for your big tournament. The same tournament I'm playing in. If you're referring to the International Gaming Olympics."

Buster's face went white. "No way you're in the tournament. Only the best in the world get invited."

"I guess that's what I am."

I reached into my wallet and flashed my registration card for the tournament. "This city kid punched his ticket weeks ago."

"All right. Let's see what kind of chops you have. I could use a warmup before the tournament. I'm sure this will be quick. Let's make it interesting. A little wager. Winner pays $15 for the cover charge."

I shook Buster's hand and agreed on the bet.

"Something else you need to know. We've played before. I'm HoodRat37 online. We've had some battles, BustingBalls58."

"How ironic. I guess I'll be pummeling you like I do every time we play."

This is the point where everything Buster says is true. I've never come close to beating him, most people never have. I've been talking like a confident gamer, which I am, but I know my audience. Then we played Mortal Kombat.

It didn't go well.

I punched, jumped, dodged, and punched some more. Buster laughed his way to three straight victories. It was like I was playing my dad and didn't know how to use the joy stick.

My mind raced to the tournament and how Buster would wipe the floor with me. After my performance in Geekon, I'd be luck to get out of the first round. My skills aren't bad, I can hang with most of the gamers in my region.

Buster was a champ for a reason. He's not intimidated by anyone.

Even trash talking city kids.

Buster shook my hand and gave an evil grin. He said good luck in the tournament and if it were him, he'd just drive back to California.

I paid the $15.

Not exactly what I had in mind for my first visit to New Mexico. Maybe another visit to a Breaking Bad location would cheer me up.

CHAPTER 8

Downtown Albuquerque and a visit to more Breaking Bad sites wouldn't ease the pain. Oh, the pain. Buster McKenna destroyed me in Mortal Kombat without breaking a sweat. If I was to win the IGO, something had to change, and quick. Not sure what that would be. Regardless, Buster appeared to be unbeatable.

Octavius spoke first, "So, big bro. I know you're a skilled gamer and have beat many opponents in your short life. But what I just saw back at the arcade makes me a little worried. I'm wondering if our road trip adventure, and the potential of never going outside again, after Dad grounds us the rest of our teenage years, is worth it. Should we just cut our losses and go home?"

"Sheesh, Octo-man. I thought you were my support and encouragement for the tournament? Work on your pep talk skills."

Edgar chimed in and mumbled under his breath, "Work on your gaming skills. Or you're getting embarrassed at the tourney."

"Hey, reality check time. I'm the one putting everything

on the line. I quit my job, lied to my dad about the trip. Even lied about the regional event to qualify for the tournament. I've wanted this more than anything in my life. And the closest people in my life are saying we should turn around? What gives?"

Octavius peeked at Edgar, who was sitting in the back seat of the Civic. Edgar glanced at his shoes, ashamed about what he'd said. "Sorry, man. What I said came out wrong. Buster destroyed you and we wanted to be honest. Octavius and I were talking. We just don't want you to get embarrassed at the tournament. That's all. Take it as the opposite of supportive, or see it as your best friend and brother caring about you, and you needing a come to Jesus moment."

"You think I'm worried about getting embarrassed? My whole life has been an embarrassment. I work a crappy job. I'm growing up without a mom. We live in a rat infested apartment in the hood and my dad can't stay employed. I drive a car with way too many miles. The only thing I've never embarrassed myself with is gaming. I don't need this kind of negativity. If you are too worried about my embarrassment, you can get out and walk home."

The sun set in the distance and the explosions of oranges and reds settled over the New Mexico desert. The desert had a peaceful effect me. I knew there was a sliver of truth in what Edgar and Octavius were saying. I'd had a sick feeling in my stomach since Buster mopped the floor with me. If the other players were half as good as the champ, I had no chance. I understood.

But I'm stubborn and you only live once, right?

"I get it. Buster whipped my butt. That doesn't mean you quit. It means you have to be better. We all have to be better. Maybe you guys can start by supporting the future IGO champ," I said, giving a wink to the guys.

"You mean Buster McKenna?" asked Octavius.

"No time for jokes... jerk wad. I'm not playing around. You both have to decide if you're with me, or against me. I can go it alone. That was the original plan, anyway. I'll drop you at the next bus station, I'm serious."

"Come on, Darius, we're the Three Amigos. Why are you being so hard on us? We're trying to paint a realistic picture of what you're up against. Think of it as reverse psychology. We use the negative to bring out the best in you."

"I appreciate your wannabe mind tricks and concern. But you're supposed to be my greatest cheerleaders. What happened to all the 'you only live once' talk? That's the only reason you're on this trip."

Octavius said in a soft tone, trying not to rile me up, "We just thought you might've given Buster a little more of a challenge. You didn't come close to winning one match."

"Get off the Buster talk. I had a bad game. I get it. You guys have a crush on him or something?"

Edgar smiled, "He's not my type. Too chubby."

"Guys... Buster isn't the only one competing in the tournament. I can hang with the other gamers. I'm the southern California regional champ. That means something, right?"

"Sure it does," Octavius said holding his crotch. "Can we stop talking? I need to pee."

"Dang, little bro. You pee every five minutes."

"I'm regretting the Super Big Gulp of Dew."

Taking a pee break wasn't a bad idea. I needed a rest from the chatter in the car. I veered off the highway and found a gas station. We'd finally made it to the Colorado border and only had a few more hours to Denver. It couldn't come soon enough as Team Darius was feeling more like a one man show with every mile driven.

"Edgar, go inside with Octavius and use the bathroom. You're no better than him with your giant Super Big Gulp of Coke. I want to make good time to Denver so we can rest up for the big week. I'm getting a few more snacks to get us to our hotel."

The aisles of the Kum and Go were filled with travelers coming and going. I grabbed a few bags of chips and a Butter Finger. A kid was playing a video game in the back of the store. He had a sour look on his face. I came up behind him and asked what he was playing.

"I don't know. Some old school game. I can't figure it out."

I scanned the title on the top panel of the machine. It was Frogger. One of the best games of the 80s. I remember playing a few times with my dad at an arcade, years back. He'd said he played it on Atari when he was younger.

I asked the kid if I could try it. I dropped a coin in the machine and gently nudged the blonde haired kid aside. He looked about ten.

"The trick is to think two moves ahead. You don't want to jump to any log. Find a path that will get you to the end. Like this..."

I hopped my green frog from log to log and dodged the cars on the highway. I saw an opening and made it all the way to the top of the screen. Victory!

The young kid stood with his jaw dropped. "You're awesome! How did you do that? I've spent five bucks on this stupid game and couldn't even get to the other side once. Thanks for the tips. What's your name?"

"Darius. I'm from California. Where you from?"

"My name is Ryan Larson. I'm from Florida. My family and I are going to Denver for a video game tournament. It's the biggest one in the world."

"International Gaming Olympics, by chance?"

The young kid's eyes bulged out of his head. "How'd you know?"

"I'm going too. I'm playing in the event."

The kid reached down to a backpack leaning against the Frogger machine. He reached in and yanked out a magazine. He flipped through the pages like looking for hidden treasure. "I knew you looked familiar. Is that you?"

The picture was of me holding up a trophy at the regional championships. "That guy looks familiar," I said, leaning over the magazine, and giving the kid a half grin.

He found a Sharpie in a side pocket. "Would you autograph my magazine? You're one of my heroes."

"Excuse me?" I asked, knowing he couldn't have said what he did.

"You're one of my heroes. The way you dominated in the regionals. I followed the tournament on YouTube. I was excited to see you play in the Olympics. This is the best day of my life."

I raised up my hands. "Don't get crazy kid. I'm nothing special. I don't want to disappoint you at the tournament."

"You will destroy in the tournament. I know it."

"Thanks, man. I kind of needed to hear some good news today. It's been a little rough getting here. At least someone believes in me," I said, signing his magazine.

The kid gave me a high five and said his folks were texting him to come back to the car. "Good luck in the tournament. I'll look for you."

I gave a thumbs up and watched him vanish out the front doors of the gas station. Octavius and Edgar came out from the back of the store, near the bathrooms. "Who was that kid?" Edgar asked.

"A fan."

"Nobody knows who you are," Octavius said.

"I have peeps all over this great land. It doesn't matter. Let's get back on the road. We have a tournament to win."

"You seem rejuvenated. Sorry about all the talk in the car earlier. I wasn't trying to be Debbie Downer. We cool?" Edgar said.

"Always. Just don't mess with me the rest of the trip and we'll be fine."

I filled the Civic with gas one last time before we pulled into Denver. I hoped my only fan would be the lucky charm I needed for the tournament.

CHAPTER 9

THE DENVER CONVENTION CENTER WAS IN THE HEART of downtown. We arrived late in the evening, the last leg a struggle to keep my eyes open. The Convention Center housed the gaming stadium for the tournament, and our rooms for lodging. We bartered with the girl at the front desk for one room with two king beds. I had no intention of spooning with my brother, or having Edgar breathing in my face all night. A king bed would keep us at proper distance.

Octavius and Edgar headed to the room for some sleep. After I got settled in the room, I wandered the halls of the Convention Center. Get a feel for the place. Take it all in. My stomach was in knots, thinking about the first round beginning in the morning. Maybe seeing where I'd be doing battle would help the nerves. I took the escalator down to the gaming stadium. Banners hung from the rafters of past champions. Jerry Smith, Dae Jong Yang, and of course, Buster McKenna's banner for all to see.

I stared straight up and imagined my name on a banner. The first African American champion of the International

Gaming Olympics. A kid from the hood a gaming champ. It sounded perfect in my head.

Unfortunately, it would take a lot of skill and luck to win this thing. I'd at least keep the dream alive in my mind for now.

I walked through the rows of booths ready for the thousands of visitors and contestants the next day. Every controller manufacturer, gaming company, and anything related to the billion-dollar gaming industry were on display.

I made my way down to the gaming stage. The contestants each had their own gaming desk with a monitor, headphones, controllers, and official game clock. Large flat screens hung all over the convention center for the audience to watch the action. One giant screen hung from the center of the stadium. A screen as big as the one at the Dallas Cowboys Stadium. I tried to imagine my face scrolling across the screen after I defeated Buster McKenna in Quake or Halo.

I found a folding chair near the front row of the tournament venue. A custodian pushed a machine and cleaned the floors. He gave a smile and continued to push the loud machine.

The low hum of the floor cleaning machine, and the noise in my mind, were a welcome break from the car ride. I noticed the cross dangling from my neck. The one my mom gave Octavius. It gave me a moment of peace. The nerves were subsiding. Things would work out as they should. I knew Mom would've supported me playing in the tournament. She didn't always understand the stuff I was into. But she always loved and supported whatever we did. That's all that mattered.

A voice roused me from my calm state.

A man with slicked back hair combed to one side and wearing a Hawaiian shirt waved a piece of paper in the air. "Darius, Darius Montgomery? I need to talk to you."

Oh crud. What did I do?

I rose from the stadium chair. "Yeah, that's me. Can I help you?"

The man wearing the Hawaiian shirt stuttered a little over his words. "I've been assigned to you. Much work to do."

"Excuse me," I said, scratching my messy hair, "I already have a team. What's this about?"

"I'm River Wild. I'll be your coach for the tournament. Think of me as your personal mentor."

"Coach? I didn't sign up for no coach."

"Every first time player in the IGO gets a coach. It's tournament policy."

I looked River up and down. He didn't exude a gamer vibe. More like a used car salesman. He had khakis pants, thinning black hair, and a gut hanging over his belt. A blazer with patches on the elbows.

Then it clicked. I'd seen this dude before. "You say your name's River Wild? The guy who won all those championships in the 80s? Man, you're a blast from the past. Pre-internet and pre-Xbox. What was that like?"

"Yes, it was a long time ago. We managed to not get eaten by dinosaurs, too. And, yes, you can still survive without a cell phone."

"That's rough."

Long before you were born, I was a champ on the Nintendo. That's probably something you've never heard of."

"The Wii is made by Nintendo. Give me some credit. I'm not just a brainless gamer. I'm a historian of the sport.

You dominated Tecmo Bowl and Mike Tyson's Punch Out. Those were your bread and butter. No one could touch you, dawg. So, you're going to coach me? You don't know the gaming world today."

River held up his credentials on a lanyard hanging around his neck. They said: Official Coach.

"This says I know what I'm talking about. And the first lesson of gaming is stay humble. You don't come into a competition and think you can live off past achievements. Every game is different and has its own challenges. Every opponent comes to the gaming desk with different skill sets. Humility is key. It's obvious we have some work to do."

I stood from my chair and raised a finger in his face. "Who do you think you are old timer? Talking about past achievements. Everyone knows about the titles you won in the 80s. But what happened in the 90s? When you got accused of cheating. You disappeared after that. How about a lesson on integrity?"

"They proved nothing. The Gaming Commission let me off the hook. I left gaming because I wasn't welcome. Despite never getting a conviction, I was blacklisted from every tournament. I went away because they forced me out. That was a long time ago. But here we are. Can we please forget about the past? You're stuck with me, so let's figure it out."

"First, I never asked for help. Second, I don't know you. This might be a nice gesture for new competitors. But I have my team in place and don't need your coaching. Isn't it kind of late in the game for that, anyway?"

"Not if you want to win."

I snickered. "I want to win. Why else would I drive across the country? To lose?"

"Everyone has their reasons for gaming."

"What are you going to teach me? You've been MIA from the sport for years. I assume you're doing this to make a few bucks. It's been a minute since you were making those gaming checks in the 80s."

River turned and pointed to a banner in the corner of the convention center. His eyes welled up. "Happiest day of my life. The day I won the IGO. The tournament was definitely not what it is today. But for a kid from Long Island, not in the popular crowd, it meant the world. I wish it opened doors for a better life. It has been anything but. Yet, for a week, I stood in the gaming ring and punched my heart out, and won. It may have been a long time ago. But I still have things to teach you, if you're willing. It starts with humility. Meet me at 5 AM in Hall B and we'll get started."

"5 AM? You kidding me? My first match isn't until ten. No way I'm getting up that early."

"We have plenty of time to get some good work in. Remember, you don't have a choice. It's policy. You don't want to forfeit the tournament, do you?"

"Your kidding me, right?"

"Nope, just following the rules. I'll see you at five, then. Remember, humility. Consider this lesson one. If you show up, I'll see it as progress."

River Wild yanked up his frumpy pants and waddled out of the convention center.

I scratched my head and wondered if what just happened was a dream. Not that I couldn't use any edge available. But River Wild from the dinosaur age of gaming didn't seem like the edge I needed. Humility? Who was he kidding? I'm a humble guy, right?

I sat back down on the stadium chair and read all the banners one more time. My name hanging in lights right next to River Wild. It seemed odd. But what if he had something to offer me? Something to get me over the hump and beat Buster McKenna? After the butt whooping earlier in the day, I needed to stay open to new ideas. What would it hurt?

I guess I didn't have a choice. 5 AM would come soon.

And Edgar still breathed in my face, despite having a king bed.

CHAPTER 10

When I told Edgar and Octavius I was leaving at 5 AM to meet River Wild they laughed. The continental breakfast at the Convention Center hotel didn't even start until 7 AM. Edgar suggested after the shellacking from Buster McKenna, a little more training would be a good idea. Jerk.

I found Hall B, an empty ballroom where River Wild held my first day of training. He wore red sweatpants with stains on the legs and a ratty tee shirt. His gut a little too large for the tiny tee. It was a white shirt which read: Classically Trained and had a picture of a Nintendo console. An appropriate shirt for an old school gamer.

River got right to business. "Ever hear of gamer's hand?"

"Good to see you too... Mr. Wild. It's early for questions. Please enlighten me. I've never heard of gamer's hand."

"It's when a gamer's hand cramps up from improper training."

"I've had that. When I play games online for hours on

end and never take a break. My hand cramps and it's hard to hold the controller. Usually Gatorade and rest does the trick. Who hasn't had that?"

River wrangled up his saggy sweatpants and pointed at my face. "Rest? Gatorade? You going to take a nappy pooh and sip Gatorade in the middle of the biggest tournament in the world? I don't think so, kid."

"Nappy pooh? Who talks like that?"

"I do, young buck. I've watched many a gamer lose matches because of gamer's hand. Ricky Nelson ring a bell?"

"No, what bell?"

"That's right, you haven't. Ricky Nelson got gamer's hand so bad they had to amputate his arm."

"That's not true."

"I made up the amputation part. But it could happen. Ricky Nelson was a promising gamer in the 80s and didn't have proper training. His hand is now permanently a claw. Vanished with all the other mediocre players."

I puffed out my chest. "I ain't no mediocre player. Who won the regionals in southern California? Yours truly..."

"That's not saying much. Mostly a bunch of locals thinking they have a shot at the big time. All you young kids think gaming is for losers, with no athletic ability. I beg to differ. You need to be strong in the body and mind, not to mention soul," River Wild said, his butt crack showing as he tended to a table with a row of glass jars.

"Crack kills, friend," I said, pointing at River. He pulled up his sweats and called me to the table of jars. "Please focus. Humility, remember. Stop pretending you know everything."

I leaned over six glass jars filled with white rice. Each

jar labeled with a name of a game in the tournament: Call of Duty, Quake, FIFA, Fortnite, DreamHack.

River pointed at each jar. "These are some games you'll play in the tournament, if you're lucky. Each round will play with your emotions, your heart and soul, and your hands. You need hands that can endure the rigor of a week-long competition. Stick both hands in the rice and squeeze. Keep doing it for one minute in each jar. When I say move, you move to the next jar."

Old school gamer guy was out of his mind. I didn't need this kind of training. I wasn't worried about gaming hand, or whatever you called it. I'd be fine. Figuring out how to beat Buster McKenna, not squeeze white rice at five in the morning, was a more pressing issue.

River shouted, "Go!"

I leapt to his command and dropped my hands into the first jar. "Squeeze with both hands. Imagine all eyes on you. The lights are blaring down on your sweaty face. You're losing and beginning to dehydrate. What are you going to do? Give in to gamer's hand? Or will you fight?"

I bought into his games. "Fight, sir," I muttered as I squeezed the rice. The muscles and tendons in my hands began to tire. I squeezed some more and moved to the next jar after he yelled, "Move!"

I scrambled to the next jar and repeated the process, realizing my hands might not be in the shape I'd like. After the fourth jar the burn in my fingers and palm was turning to cramping. "It will burn, young man. Keep going and don't think about the pain. The tournament is about survival and making it to the end. Most gamers win, not because of knowledge or strategy or skills in a game, they win because they train their mental and physical bodies for enduring the battle of a tournament. Your body will break down. Your mind will fail you. But how will you respond to adversity? Don't be a loser, Darius. No gamer's hand for you, no, sir."

I moved to the last jar and sweat poured down my face. Not only were my hands getting tired, but my legs were getting sore from running to each station. I had no idea how bad of shape I was in. Basketball season had ended in the spring, I guess I had been playing too many video games, and eating too many Doritos.

"Stop!" River shouted. He came over with a bottled water and some ice. "Drink the water and place the ice on your hands. You're going to want to do this after every match. Most kid's won't, and they'll pay. They'll go eat Funyuns and drink Mountain Dew. Guess where they'll end up?"

"Not sure. Humor me."

"Last place. You want to be last, or first? Win the whole thing?"

"Win."

"That's right. You either win or you lose. There's no happy middle."

"A top finish would be cool."

"Come on, Darius, you're not a loser. You came here to win, right? Erase that top finish language from your vocabulary."

"Yes, sir."

"That's more like it. Lesson one, humility. Lesson two, how to fight off gamer's hand. One more lesson before you start today's matches."

"This is feeling a lot like Karate Kid."

"Humility... please don't interrupt me," River said.

I pretended to zip my lip.

"Not only do gamers need to know the physical challenges of their matches, they also need to deal with a cluttered mind. Please come over here and lay on the yoga mat."

I stood over the mat and glanced down. "This is weird. Can I go back to bed now?"

"Get on the floor... humility...."

I obliged and settled on the floor.

"Now, the mind is a funny thing. When you're playing the best players in the world your mind must be free of distractions. Your mind is the gateway into the heart. The heart is the seed of our will and actions. If your mind gets distracted and stressed, it will lead to negative emotions. Which leads to bad decisions. We don't want that. Take a deep breath and try to clear your mind."

"Clear," I said, closing my eyes.

"Good. Now try to imagine the worst day of your life."

"What? That doesn't sound like a way to declutter the mind."

"Do it."

I traveled in my mind to the day my mom took her last breath in the hospital. My dad, brother, and some other extended family were at her bedside. Our pastor had just left after praying for her and the family. The doctors had told us there would only be a few more hours left.

"What do you see?"

"My family. The day my mother died from cancer."

"Sorry about your loss. Now let your mind go wherever it needs to wander. Let your emotions go."

I tried to revisit that awful day with my mom, but something blocked the memories. They were fuzzy. Yet, one detail stood out. I didn't cry when my mom died. I was stoic, despite everyone else in the room bawling their eyes out. What did that mean? Was I dead inside?

"What do you see? Anything jump out?"

"Yeah, I'm not crying. Why would you not cry when your mom's about to die? What's wrong with me?"

"Let the memory take you where you need to go. Let your emotions come as they will."

I was getting uncomfortable. Something in me confused about being emotionally absent when my mom was dying. I guess I'd never dealt with the pain all that well. I believed Mom would be healed, and this wasn't the end. Maybe it was some kind of protective mechanism.

River said, "Let the pain go. Let it be what it is. Don't dwell on it and take the pain or joy, just let it be."

Those words from River were comforting. My mind was letting the painful past go. I felt a sense of freedom. Of release. But then the emotions of the moment changed. I was losing the image of my mother and didn't want her face in the hospital bed to disappear. "Come back, Mom, come back."

I shot up from the yoga mat and shouted at River. "Why are we doing this? I'm here to play in a video game tournament and you're getting all Doctor Phil on me. I'm going back to my room and will see you later. Stop with all your Mr. Miyagi training. I'm leaving."

"Darius, I know this is painful. We all have regrets and hurts of the past. Free your mind and don't make this tournament bigger than it needs to be. I'm trying to help you win."

"I don't give a crap. I'm fine. See you later."

I stormed out of the convention center hall and found a coffee shop.

Sipped a vanilla latte and thought about the weird training, and Mom.

I never cried... what does that mean?

I couldn't dwell on the psychobabble stuff. I had to get ready to win an opening match of the tournament. The coffee cup in my hand trembled, and I noticed more veins coming out on my hands than before. Is it possible my hands got stronger?

CHAPTER 11

EDGAR AND OCTAVIUS MADE IT TO THE CONTINENTAL breakfast around eight. I met them for massive amounts of cereal, waffles, eggs, and bacon. We needed real food after loading up on beef jerky, Mountain Dew, and Slim Jims on the road.

I told them about the unorthodox training from River Wild. My face still red from shedding tears from thinking about Mom. "Are you crying?" Edgar asked.

"No, jerk. It's part of the healing process. River said it was good for emptying the mind of distractions."

"That sounds like a bunch of nonsense. How does crying your eyes out and thinking about sad stuff empty your mind? Seems like it would have the opposite effect. What were you thinking about?" Octavius asked.

"Mom. You remember me crying when she died?"

Octavius munched on Fruit Loops. With a mouth full of cereal. and milk dripping from his face, he said, "I don't know, man. I was little."

"Little? It was a few years ago."

"True. Sorry I don't keep tabs on whether my brother is

a crier. I have better things to do. You most likely cried. We all did."

"I don't think I did. When River made me bring up a painful memory of the past. I had this fuzzy memory of not crying in the hospital when she died. Everyone was bawling, expect me. What the heck does that mean?"

Edgar leaned back in his chair and gnawed on a slice of bacon. "Our brains are complex. Memories even more odd. You ever try to bring up a memory before kindergarten? Sometimes you're positive the memory is vivid and you can remember the details like it was yesterday. But in reality, someone told you about the experience and you chalked it up as your own. The mind is a mystery. I wouldn't worry about it. Why do you care so much?"

"I don't know. River Wild is apparently my coach for the tournament. An old school gamer with some weird training tactics. I'm just following his orders. Said I'd be disqualified if I didn't have a mentor. The mind games are supposed to free me up. Remove distractions. Help me become a champion."

"Is it helping?"

"Don't know, yet. But I obviously needed to get some stuff out. I feel a little better."

Edgar licked the rest of his plate clean and then pulled out a program for the tournament. He read the bio of my first opponent: Chris Larson. "Whatever mind tricks you need to win your first match, do it. You're playing a dude from Mississippi. He's supposedly a master at Counter Strike. No worries, player. You got this."

The name sounded familiar.

I snapped my fingers.

Chris Larson was active in online gaming communities. I remember played the guy and beating him. Larson had skills, like most of the contestants, but I was confident I could take him down in the first round. Counter Strike was a first player shooter game where counter-terrorist agents try to stop terrorists from doing, well, acts of terror. It's a fast-paced game of detonating bombs, shooting bad guys, and saving the world. My kind of game.

The first round of the tournament is a timed event. Which means you play for a period and when the buzzer sounds the player with the most points wins. I like these events because they force you to play aggressive.

I wore my Carver High School basketball jersey over a tee shirt, and some jogging pants. I enjoyed being comfortable when playing in tournaments. The stress and lights make you hot. Also, I like having the good luck charm of my high school b-ball jersey.

River Wild came huffing and puffing to the registration table. A young girl flipped through sheets of paper. "Darius Montgomery. He's going to be your next champ," he said, as the girl scanned the official registration sheet. River gave a wink and slicked a wispy strand of what was left of his hair over his balding head.

"You'll be playing Chris Larson in arena four. To our left," she said, handing me the official International Gaming Olympics lanyard. I gave it a brief squeeze, like rubbing a rabbit's foot.

"You ready, kid? Remember, stay humble. And if your head gets full of negative thoughts, remember the breathing and talking techniques I showed you."

"Yes, I remember. You're awesome, Darius. No one can beat you, Darius. Got it, good."

Octavius and Edgar tried to hold down their laughter. They excused themselves, gave me a high five, and found a seat in the stands.

I took one more deep breath and found my seat at a gaming cubicle. It was a desk, an oversized chair, a monitor, and a headset. I glanced at Chris, who was a tall and slender kid with a nice smile. He didn't seem all that intimidating.

The announcer came over the loud speakers. "Ladies and gentlemen, boys and girls. Welcome to the first round of the International Gaming Olympics. We have a treat for you today. Hailing from Los Angeles California, and the southern California regional champ, Darius Montgomery." The crowd erupted in applause and shouting. The moment of the room, with thousands of people screaming my name, gave me a nauseous stomach. I liked the support of the fans, but it made me nervous. What if I fail? What if I stink it up like I did against Buster? My head was full of negative thoughts. Does Dad know I'm gone? I breathed and said the mantra: Darius, you're a champ. It wasn't helping, and I sounded stupid.

The announcer continued, "And to my left is another champ. The regional champ in Mississippi, who's a master at Counter Strike... Chris Larson." The crowd erupted, and Chris gave a pleasant wave.

We put on our headsets and I took one last deep breath. I caressed the cross necklace and said a prayer. A giant screen wrapped around the gaming stadium almost a full three hundred and sixty degrees. What we saw on our monitors was what the fans saw on the wraparound screen. People screamed my name and Chris'. It was hard to concentrate. This event was three times larger than the regionals. It was a different animal, playing in your bedroom online versus playing in front of thousands of people.

"Ladies and gentlemen, the format of Counter Strike is simple. Whoever has the most points when the buzzer sounds is the winner. Contestants, grab your controllers and let's rumble."

The screens lit up, and we started tapping our controllers.

Music thumped and people cheered.

Once the game began, all the noise dissipated. When you're in the moment of a tournament you forget the opponent. It's you and your screen and not much else. All I could see out of the corner of my eye was a giant clock on the wall, counting down fifteen minutes.

My counter-terrorist character set a bomb in a bombed out building.

Chris set one.

We traded attacks for the entire fifteen minutes. I could see a video of him in the corner of my screen. He was sweating and wiping his brow. I managed a double digit lead with five minutes to go. I think he even cursed under his breath at one point.

I settled into a groove and was finding and detonating bombs all over the map of the game. My points shot up and people yelled my name.

Then it happened.

My right hand, the one opposite the joystick, began to cramp. I fought off the cramps and tried to grind out the last three minutes. My hand was curling up in a ball. I stretched the hand back and forth and tried to get it to come back to a normal shape. All I could think of was Gatorade and a nap and River yelling at me.

Chris set off three bombs and stopped a group of terrorists, and my lead dwindled. We were only a thousand points apart.

The clock said two minutes.

My hand was not in good shape. Stupid River Wild was right. Gamer's hand is no joke.

A horn blasted.

The clock hit zero. I won by one hundred points.

I rose to shake Chris' hand with the non-cramped one. "Good match. You're a good player," I said, leaving the gaming arena to find my guys.

River Wild snuck up behind me. "You cramped up, didn't you?"

"Nope. My hand is just sore. I'll be fine. It happens."

"You got gamer's hand didn't you? I told you. These tournaments are not like your little regional events. The stress and noise and chaos is a different animal. You barely won that match. Consider yourself lucky."

"I'm not going to lie... hearing your name chanted from the rafters is awesome. But the environment is intense. I wasn't ready for the distractions of the noise and all the lights. It's a bit much."

"Remember, kid, it's not about how skilled you are in the games. Manage the chaos and the unknowns of the environment. Chris was just as good a player as you, but you managed the chaos a little better than him. Barely. Be warned, it will not get any easier from here on out."

River handed me an ice pack and an Ace bandage. "Put this on your claw. Hydrate and keep stretching those fingers. You will not win this thing if your hand is a useless crab claw."

I wrapped the ice and bandage around my hand. "Thanks for the confidence. I'll be fine."

"Humility. Lesson two, gamer's hand is real. Lesson three, manage the chaos."

"Thanks, Yoda," I said, holding my claw.

"You make jokes, but there are hundreds of contestants

here that want it more than you. You squeaked by a very winnable first round opponent. I'm proud of you, but don't get cocky. And, yes, I am Yoda, don't forget it," River said with a smile.

"Rest up for the next match, kid. Get something to eat and rest that hand," River said, and disappeared into the crowds.

Edgar and Octavius ran down from the stands and slapped me on the back. "Dude, you won. How was it? It was a close match."

"Good, I think. My hand kind of hurts, but I think I'll be ready for the next opponent. Who do I play?"

Octavius stared at a scoreboard hanging from the celling. "Don't know yet. Still waiting for the first round to end."

"I'm resting until the next event. You guys want to hang out?"

They agreed.

My phone buzzed in my pocket.

Then it happened. Sooner than expected. My dad texted me, wondering where I was.

So much for keeping an empty mind.

CHAPTER 12

We headed back to the hotel room, and I strategized what to say to Dad. Do I text back? Go dark and not respond? Board a plane to Mexico, change my name, and live out my days on the beach? I saw it in a movie once.

I sweated through my IGO shirt, and not from the Denver heat. It was mild for June. No, the extra perspiration was Dad's parenting sixth sense activated, and I was going down. Hard. What do I do?

We entered the hotel room, and I jammed my phone in Octavius' face. "Little bro, call Dad. You were supposed to stay home. None of this would've happened if you'd stuck to the plan. You owe me."

Octavius paced the room and held up a hand. "I owe you nothing. No time for blame. Maybe it's nothing. Dad calls and texts all the time. Let's not lose our minds here."

I leapt from the bed and banged my head against the wall. "I don't need this right now. River said you need a free mind, or something. If not, you're going to lose every match. I don't want to lose... The thought of Dad finding out is haunting my brain."

Edgar enjoyed the meltdown like a candle in the New Mexico desert. "Friend, you need to chill the heck out. It's one text message. I'm not sure how you read texts, but they don't always mean anything. Hit him back and stop losing your mind, kid."

It could be nothing, right? I stared at my iPhone and imagined Dad's face coming out of the screen with flames shooting from his eyes. *I'm watching you, Darius. I'm always watching you. Why aren't you working at the golf course and helping the family? I'm very disappointed...*

I tossed the phone on the bed. "Nope. I can't do it. Dad will flip. Octavius, you have to do it. Text him back."

Octavius gave a sigh. "Really, dude? Darius Montgomery, the next IGO champ, and he fears texting his dad. How are you going to stay composed when Buster McKenna is kicking your butt all over the gaming stadium?"

"I'll be fine. Tell Dad work is good and Edgar and I are headed to a movie. He won't think anything of it. Just text him what I tell you."

Octavius rolled his eyes and tapped on the screen.

Darius: *hey pops, work was good yesterday. I made lots of tips. I'm headed to the movies with Edgar. Talk soon.*

Octavius hit send, and we waited. The thirty seconds before Dad responded felt like nine hours.

Dad: *Good to hear about the tips. Every bit helps. I talked to a friend at a landscaping company. They have a position open. I start tomorrow.*

. . .

Darius: *Sweet! I knew you'd find another job. Have a great first day and I'll see you soon.*

The news of Dad getting a job was like a giant weight had been lifted. All that guilt for quitting my job. Now he could make some money and keep the family afloat.

I put the phone on a charger and told Octavius the news.

"I told you, big bro. You just need to calm down. Take it easy. Things always work out the way they're supposed to. Dad is clueless about our little road trip. Aren't you happy about the job? You can stop freaking out about the money stuff and focus on winning the tournament," Octavius said, finding a remote and flipping on the TV.

"The money stuff is still real. It's not like Dad won the lottery. We're still poor. But at least I'm not the sole provider any longer."

Octavius lounged on the bed and Edgar fought him for the remote. He didn't hear what I said.

When you get older, you realize how much money your parents spend on things that seem lame to kids. Things like insurance, gas for the car, rent, and utilities. All these expenses add up. Wanting to grow up fast no longer seemed like a good idea. No wonder our families are so stressed out all the time. Despite my dad finding work, those bills didn't pay themselves. I had to win the tournament to pay off stacks of medical bills, or we'd continue to sneak by every month.

I sat on the edge of the bed and thanked God for the good news of the job. I didn't want Edgar and Octavius to know what I was doing, so I just said a prayer in my head. From a young age I sensed that life was too mysterious and complex and hard for stuff to be just random chance. Something or someone was watching out for us.

Edgar stopped yelling at Octavius for the remote long enough to slap me on the back. "Dude, so happy about pops finding a job. Now you can focus on the tournament. You have about an hour until the next match."

I thanked Edgar and tried to refocus my mind on the task at hand. "Don't tell me my opponent this time. I think that was a bad strategy last time. I want to go in with a clear mind, ready to kick butt."

Edgar nodded and tossed the tournament program on the bed. My phone buzzed on the charger. I picked it up and checked the text message.

It was Dad.

Dad: *My car died. I need a ride to my job tomorrow. It's across town. Can you pick me up at 8 AM?*

So much for a clear mind.

CHAPTER 13

DAD FORGOT I HAD WORK AT THE GOLF COURSE FIRST thing in the morning. No way I could give him a lift to the new job. His friend Mario would take him. I dodged a bullet, but the fear of getting caught returned. Not good timing for my next match, which began in less than ten minutes.

River Wild reached for my hands and gave them a look over. "You ice and stretch like I said?"

"Yes, sir. Hands are good. I think I was putting a death grip on the controller in the first match. Probably nerves. I get grippy when I'm anxious. I'll try to chill out this time."

"Grippy? Not sure that's a thing, but not a bad idea to chill out. You're going to need your A Game. Every match from here on out gets harder and harder. Each opponent more experienced. I don't want you taking a quick exit because of gamer's hand or diarrhea."

"Diarrhea?"

"It happened to me. For another time."

River flipped through the tournament program, which had a list of all the participants in the IGO. He flopped the program on the table. He pointed at a name. "Here's your next opponent."

I covered the face of the guy on the page and looked away. "I don't want to see my next opponent. New strategy."

"Ok... what will that do?"

"It does no good seeing my next opponent. In my first match, I was overconfident. Most of these guys I've met through online gaming sessions, or read about in Gamer Addict. I want to play with a free mind. No expectations and no fear. Whether I've beat them in the past, it doesn't matter."

River Wild placed his dark-rimmed glasses on the bridge of his nose. He nodded and forced a smile. I could tell it impressed him with my somewhat mature new strategy. Was I becoming humble after all? He closed the program. "Great strategy, kid, I see growth. Humility. I like it. Well, you'll hear your opponent over the loudspeaker soon enough. Did I mention your next game is an old school one? One of my favorites. Mortal Kombat."

My heart sank. Not because of drawing Mortal Kombat. I'm not bad with the old school version. The newer Play Station 4 version is a lot more fun, in my humble opinion. I guess getting destroyed by Buster McKenna in MK caused some PTSD. I had the image fresh in my mind of Buster laughing at me with his little friends in New Mexico. All I dwelled on was watching his character pound my face in, over and over.

Not the free mind I'd hoped for.

"What's the matter? Are you not comfortable with Mortal Kombat?" River asked.

"MK is no problem. It's complicated."

"Sorry, kid. No time for complicated. It's game time."

The announcer came over the speaker and the lights dimmed. "Welcome back to the gaming stadium. How's everyone doing? The tournament has been exciting. Some expected victories and some upsets. Well, the second round won't disappoint. We have another doozy for you in just a moment. One quick announcement: please don't use the bathroom near the main concession stand. We think someone might've had too many chili dogs... use your imagination."

The crowd groaned, which then turned into laughter.

"With no further ado. Let me welcome our next competitors to the stage. From LA LA Land, let's give a warm IGO welcome to Darius Montgomery," the crowd erupted. I was loving this part.

"His opponent, all the way from South Korea, William Chen. Fasten your seat belts and get ready to go to combat. Mortal Kombat..."

The crowd cheered and my stomach did a backflip. I thought about Buster's fat face and him laughing as his belly rolls danced in time. The disappointment in Dad's voice in LA after learning I had lied to him about going to Denver. He would find out eventually. I couldn't fight off my busy mind.

I took a deep breath and glanced at River. He mouthed the word: *relax*.

Our monitors lit up and techno music thumped through the stadium. The giant screen which wrapped around the stadium showed our two characters, ready to battle. I chose Scorpion and Chen chose Smoke. Smoke, a ninja who turned from an assassin to a cyborg. Scorpion, the ultimate anti-hero. Fighting for good and yet had a dark side. I resonated with the character. I'd had good luck with Scorpion in the past and felt confident he'd get me to the winner's circle.

The format of the MK match is a best of five series. Whoever wins three matches first is the winner. No points, no time, just a battle to the death.

In the fighting games you have to feel out your opponent. But not for too long. You want to see what kind of skills they have. Take too long and you lose in quick succession.

I gripped the controller and glanced at William Chen, who was short and chunky. He had a serious face. I gave a couple stretches of my hands and prayed they didn't end up in claws.

"Ready... fight!" the announcer yelled.

The crowd burst into hooting and hollering.

I tapped the controller and danced Scorpion around the ring, dodging a couple punches to the face. I could tell Chen was checking my moves out, too. I jumped to the left and landed a roundhouse kick across Smoke's face. Chen glanced in my direction and gave a nod like 'not a bad move, kid'.

It was obvious I was one of the younger kids in the tournament. The cutoff was sixteen, and for good reason. Chen looked like he was an accountant with five kids, living in the suburbs with a Volvo.

Chen landed a sharp jab to my head. Blood splattered across the screen. Our power bars were about even, with half left. I jumped up and did a special move reserved for Scorpion. He came down with a spear jab and landed a blow to the head of Smoke. He wobbled, and we heard the sweetest words in all the universe: finish him!

I did just that and applied a finisher move. Scorpion came up to Smoke, ripped off his mask, his face then turned to a skeleton. Scorpion breathed fire and Smoke turned to ash. Kind of awesome, and gory, if you think about it.

The crowd went wild.

One match for Darius, none for Chen.

Chen slapped the side of his screen and tossed his headphones on the desk. He almost knocked the monitor to the gaming stadium floor. I had Chen where I wanted him. Frustrated, and a head full of doubt. The crowd roared with applause and the extra noise was fuel for carrying me to the finish line. Octavius, Edgar, and River gave a point in my direction. I was getting more comfortable with the chaos of the gaming stadium with each match.

I'd forgotten the weight of the tournament. Gaming had that affect. I could lose myself and forget the pain of the world for a moment.

I was operating in that gaming zone where everything is clear. Every move is exact and precise and your mind just reacts. Clear enough to take the next match. And the next one.

Chen done. Game over.

I shook Chen's hand. He barely looked me in the eye and had a tear welling up in the corner. Maybe Chen missed home and needed to kiss his wife and five kids. Drive home in the Volvo, who knows?

My team ran onto the gaming stadium platform and gave me a hug. River stood back and didn't look that excited that I'd made quick work of Chen.

I glanced up at the official scoreboard and saw my name in third place for total points. River glanced up, too, and shook his head.

"What's up, man? Looks like your grandma died. I did it, I destroyed that dude."

"Every tournament will have those kinds of matches. Not good for the ego."

"What do you mean? My mind was clear, and I didn't get my hand locked up. Why are you so down? I'm in third place for the entire tournament. What the heck, man? I thought you'd be more excited for me. What do you want from me?"

"Easy wins give you false hope. Only champs get this. You believe you're better than you are. Second round matches are a crap shoot. Chen's opponent in the first round a mystery. He could've of beat someone with little experience. You don't know."

"Who cares? I won. That's all that matters, right? A win's a win."

"Humility and playing the right way matters. Don't think beating some middle-level gamer proves anything. Enjoy the win, just don't let your ego get inflated."

I stared at the floor as the crowds died down. I didn't know what to say. You win and it's not enough. Why is River so negative? I'm just happy to be here. I didn't have time for his negativity.

I glared at River. "You can sulk in the corner. I will enjoy the win with the rest of the team."

River didn't speak and disappeared into the crowds.

CHAPTER 14

We spent the afternoon at the hotel pool. The next round wouldn't begin until the next morning, and we had the rest of the day free. I had no idea how tired I'd get playing video games. The stress of performing in front of a screaming crowd, and the pressure to win the tournament, was wearing me out. Not to mention the pressure to provide for the family was an added weight of weariness. Kids play video games, eat pizza, find dates, and work crappy summer jobs. Not worry about money problems.

Octavius and Edgar wrestled at one end of the pool and I floated on a raft on the other. Some contestants in the tournament had afternoon matches, which explained the empty pool. The air was warm and the lapping sound of the water against the raft was soothing. Octavius paddled away from Edgar and tried to tip over my raft. So much for a moment of solace.

"Come on, jerk," I yelled at Octavius, who swam to the edge, laughing. I recovered the raft and climbed back on top. Octavius held onto the edge of the pool. "I'm proud of you, big bro. You're kicking butt and taking names in the tourney. How you doing?"

"Good, I guess. Except River was acting weird after my last win."

"Why was he so upset?" Octavius asked.

I covered my eyes with my left hand as the sun blasted my face. "I don't know. Something about getting too confident. My ego getting inflated. Some kind of mind trick motivation. A weird psychology strategy for helping me win."

Octavius made a sour face. "Weird, right? Who cares? A win is a win. What's that about?"

"I won't let it bother me. River Wild is an old school guy and means well. He doesn't understand our generation. We don't respond well to criticism. Probably says something about us. Regardless, a win is a win. Any contact from Dad?"

"Not since yesterday when he needed a ride. Should we call him? He won't suspect anything if we strike first. Thoughts?"

"Not a bad idea. Give a casual call or text and see how his first day went. It would be a nice gesture. I miss the old man, anyway."

"Me, too. Let's call him when we get back to the room."

Edgar swam over to the raft and joined in the conversation. "What you buttheads talking about?"

"Your mom. How she still calls you Eddie Bear."

"Don't say that again. I have a reputation to keep. I'm hoping to find a nice girl here at the tournament. They can't know my mom's pet name."

"Reputation? You weren't doing well with the ladies in LA. It will not be any different in Colorado. Eddie Bear could help your cause. It wouldn't hurt."

Edgar tackled the raft and punched me in the side.

"Okay, I'll stop. Take it easy. I have a competition to win. I can't break my hand... Eddie Bear."

Edgar jammed my face in the water. "You're lucky I'm not playing in the tourney. You'd be out already."

I spit water out of my mouth and wiped water from my eyes. "That's the funniest thing I've heard in a while. Do you even know how to hold a controller?"

Edgar climbed onto the raft and waved off my comment. "Whatever, dude. For what it's worth, we're proud of you. You're hanging with the best, living the dream. Right?"

I hesitated. I couldn't answer the question. My thoughts were conflicted. I just responded with whatever came to mind. "Heck, yeah, coolest experience of my life. But to be honest... I thought I'd feel different. It's like something inside won't let me enjoy the experience to the full. Maybe it's the guilt of lying to my dad. I'm supposed to enjoy being a kid, you know? We will be seniors and kings of the school next fall. Too much adult stuff to worry about."

"I get it. My folks are always talking about getting into college and finding good jobs. Is that all life is? We're supposed to bust our butts in college, rack up huge debts, and then work jobs we hate. Is there more? Man, sorry, this is getting deep."

"I get it. Happiness can be so fleeting. Here for a second and gone in a heartbeat. I beat Chen and had a moment of euphoria. And then two seconds later River is telling me not to be happy, or get a big head. Takes the wind out of your sails. Maybe that's how life is, and I'm expecting too much."

Edgar bumped my fist. "Well, let's enjoy the moment. That's all we got. You have a third round match tomorrow. A few more wins and you will get to the final four. Let's enjoy the ride. You only live once, right?"

"Yep," I said, leaping onto the raft and slamming Edgar underwater. "Now it's time to die, Mr. Swamp."

We swam for the rest of the afternoon until sundown. We played and laughed and did what kids do. It was good to forget about the tournament, or Dad or money or even River Wild, for an afternoon.

We headed to a Taco Bell down the road and brought food back to the room to watch a movie. There was a Die Hard marathon, which were some of our favorite action movies. We ate and farted. Okay, Edgar did most of the farting, but it lightened the mood.

We watched John McClane leap from a building and we all cheered. He's a tough dude.

I reached to the night stand and checked the time on my phone. It was an hour behind in LA, making it 8 PM. I wondered what Dad was up to. Hoping his new job was working out.

Right then my phone buzzed. It was a text from Dad.

How are you, son? Missing you. First day at the new job was good.

Weird when that happens. You're thinking of someone and they call.

I wrote back. *Doing good. Work has been crazy. Probably going to stay one more night at Edgar's. We are going to a pool party at Reggie's. Picked up another shift at the course. Every bit helps, right?*

Dad said, *Sounds good. Come home sometime tomorrow. We can have dinner.*

The lies piled up like smog hovering over downtown LA. They were there and hanging like a dark cloud. I wanted to tell the truth, but couldn't. Wouldn't? Hard to tell the difference. My motivation for winning this tournament blurrier with every passing hour. One moment it's for noble reasons to help the family out of a financial bind. Other times it's pride and ego. Is River right? My ego is inflated like a giant pool raft? A gaming champ for no other reason than to boast to other kids. Be cool? Get a date? I'm a conflicted soul, wondering why I'm here. What does it all mean?

I panicked with the last text from Dad. I called Octavius over and showed him the message. "Oh, crap. That's not good. What are you going to say?" Octavius asked.

"Well, I can't say sure, I'll bring the pizza. What do I do, man? I'm freaking out."

"Tell him you'll text later and keep him posted. You have some stuff to take care of. Not sure if you can do dinner. He won't think anything of it."

"That sounds like a recipe for disaster. Dad will know something is up if I keep dodging his requests. He's going to show up here and give us all spankings."

"I think you're building this up in your head. Calm down. Come up with a better idea, then."

"Fine."

I sent the text and said I'd let him know the next day.

Dad responded, *Is everything okay?*

I said, *Yep, just have to run a couple errands.*

I laid my head on the pillow and stared at the ceiling.

Die Hard blared in the background. Gunshots and John McClane yelling "Yippe kaye..."

Dad said, *Okay, chat tomorrow.*

"I'm a dead man," I said, folding my hands over my head.

"We're all going to be dead if Dad finds out," Octavius said, staring at the giant flat-screen TV.

"I'm the one living off church camp money. You're at least doing this for more pure reasons."

"True, you're still going to hell," I said, with a snort.

"I don't need that kind of guilt," Octavius said.

I started to drift off to sleep.

There was a knock on the door. Octavius needed more food and had ordered a pizza.

"Get the door. Do you ever get full?" I asked. "How do you stay so slim?"

"Genetics."

A voice yelled out. "Darius Montgomery. Can you please come to the door?"

"Did you use my name for the pizza? I'm not paying."

"Not important right now... Just get it, I'll pay you back. I'm too into the movie."

I got up and opened the door.

CHAPTER 15

I IMAGINED A BALD, MIDDLE-AGED MAN MATCHING THE baritone voice. Instead, there were two skinny men wearing black hoodies and Colorado Rockies hats, leaned against the wall in the hallway. One smoked a cigarette, and the other had his arms crossed and stared off into space, appearing uninterested.

I closed the hotel door behind me. Certain they found the wrong room and weren't the pizza guys. "Can I help you?"

The man smoking tossed the cigarette on the carpet and stomped it out. "You know what you did?"

I scratched my frizzy hair and tried to think if we'd broken some rule in the tournament. Running at the hotel pool, always a possibility. "Can I have more details? I'm sure whatever it is we can make it right."

"Not possible. What you have can't be erased."

I could sense this conversation was heading nowhere good. These dudes stared off into the distance like they weren't there intellectually. They smelled, too. "Please be more specific, or I'm heading back to the room. I have some friends in there and don't want to keep them waiting."

The aloof guy in the hoodie leaning against the wall spoke up, "Is it hard?"

"Is what hard? Stop playing games. I need to go," I said, turning back to the hotel door.

He grabbed my shoulder and spun me toward his face. "Is it hard being black?"

"Excuse me? You didn't say what I think you said? Is it hard being ignorant?"

The cigarette smoker chuckled and took a deep hit on the cancer stick. "Your people are the ignorant ones. A drain on society."

I took a deep breath and tried to stay calm. Not the first time an ignorant person said something stupid. I had to decide whether to punch the guy in the face or do the smart thing and walk away. I'd spent my entire life dealing with the voices of ignorant people who don't understand the cultural story of the black community. Dad always said when at all possible, just walk away. Violence leads nowhere good.

"Here's the deal. Everything in me wants to punch a hole in your face. But you'd be a waste of time and energy. Ignorant people just want you to react and respond to their idiocy. Not going to happen. I need to get back to my friends."

The smoker slammed his fist against the wall of the hallway. A picture of a beach hanging on the wall tilted to the left. He leaned on top of me and whispered. "Take it back."

"Take what back?" I said, trying to avoid the rancid breath of the smoker.

"I didn't like what you said. You can't hurt us. We're the

superior race. Take it back, calling me ignorant. I have more smarts in my pinky than in your entire body."

I turned my head and held every ounce of anger back so as not to punch the fool. "I'm sorry. Go take your smart pinky with your boyfriend and let me get back to my guests."

Before I could respond the man reared back and punched me in the gut. It knocked the air from my stomach. As I bent over, trying to find air and yell for help, the other guy dropped an elbow on the back of my head. I didn't black out, but felt immense pain in my head and ear.

Then, like a well-rehearsed dance recital, one guy pulled out a hard object. A bar. He was going after the money maker. Amid the chaos of arms and legs flying everywhere, he grabbed my hand. He smashed it repeatedly with the hard object. And slammed it against the wall. When I fell to the ground, the other guy tried to stomp my other hand, but I protected it under my limp body.

My money maker. Anything but the hand for an aspiring gaming champion. Then, like that, they ran down the hall and disappeared into the night. I lay with a battered face and a thumb I could barely move.

Edgar eased the door open as I laid in the hallway writhing in pain. Octavius came, too. They picked me up, ushered me into the room, and placed my broken body on the bed. "What the heck happened?" Edgar asked, racing to the bathroom for a cloth to wipe off the blood on my face and ear.

"Some dudes jumped me in the hallway."

"What?" Octavius asked.

"Yeah, some guys were talking trash. Then they beat the crap out of me."

"We heard thumping in the hallway and came to see what it was."

"Yeah, thanks for the speedy response."

"Sorry, man, we thought it was the pizza guy. You were chatting him up."

Edgar wiped blood from my ear and tapped down the cuts on my battered hand. It was swelling. My thumb was in bad shape. Octavius looked at the thumb. "Not good, big bro. That's the money maker."

"You're telling me."

"What did those guys want?"

"Not sure. But that was a planned beating. Attacked my hand with a club or something. Calling me all kinds of racist names."

"Really? So many idiots in the world. You think they beat you up because you're black?"

"That, and someone didn't want me gaming anymore. I guess this is the end of the tournament."

"Don't say that."

"The tournament is over. I can't play without a thumb. I'll tell River Wild I'm done and we'll leave first thing in the morning. Probably better anyway. If we leave soon, Dad won't ever know what happened," I said, trying to stretch my hand, with little progress.

Octavius sat on the edge of the bed, silent. He shook his head and wiped his eyes. He was crying. "I hate this world. People are so mean. They just destroyed your dreams all because of the color of our skin. Who does that kind of thing?"

I tossed the cloth on the bed and snuggled up next to my little bro. "Hey, don't worry about me. We have each other and that's all that matters. I'll find a new dream.

There is always next year. Maybe I wasn't ready for the bigness of the moment. It's okay, little man."

"Still sucks."

"Yeah, it does. But we can either get bitter or better. I'm choosing to be the bigger man. If we give in to the idiots of the world, they win. Right?"

"Sure, I guess. But I want you to win the tournament. Can you see how you feel in the morning?"

I glanced down at my banged up hand. "My face is a mess, but I can play with a shiner and a few cuts. The hand is a problem. My thumb could be broken. I don't think that'll heal overnight."

"How about you ice it with the hotel bucket? You believe in miracles? Do it for me?"

"Man, little bro. You want this bad. More than me."

"Why are you giving in so easy?"

"I'm not. I just don't know what to do with a gimpy hand," I said, examining the injured thumb.

"You've played through worse. Remember when you fractured your wrist in basketball? You still played in that local tournament with a cast. Don't give up..."

"That was different. My fingers still worked. Right now these little piggies aren't good. Thumb barely moves. I'll make you a deal. Let's sleep on it. That's all we can do. I'll give River Wild a heads up."

Octavius left for the bathroom and came back with an ice bucket. He ran out the door and was back in a few minutes. He had the bucket filled with ice. "Put that hand in here," he said, pointing to my mangled thumb.

I did as he said. It felt good for a little while before the hand got numb. Octavius had turned into my personal trainer. I knew he was always my biggest fan. But I'd never seen him want me to stay in a tournament more than what he showed in the hotel room.

There was a knock on the door. We all looked at one another and waited.

A second knock.

A voice yelled out, "Papa John's. I have a deliver for Darius Montgomery."

We all sighed in relief.

"Pizza is on me tonight, guys," Edgar said, opening the door, tipping the delivery guy, and saying goodbye.

We ate our pizza, finished Die Hard, and didn't talk about what happened in the hallway. I let River Wild know what happened, and he suggested waiting until morning. See how my hand responded to the ice and rest. I also called the hotel lobby to tell them what had happened in the hallway. They had no cameras in the hall and were not much help. River would let the Gaming Commission know. They would investigate, but it was unlikely they'd find much.

I finished my pizza and began to daydream. The anger was pent up and more ravenous than what I'd let on to Edgar and Octavius. If I saw those hooded guys again, I might regret what I'd do or say.

I guess the good thing about dreams is you can find another one. But this dream was a hard one to let die.

CHAPTER 16

RIVER WILD HAD ME COME UP TO HIS ROOM ON THE third floor first thing in the morning. My hand was sore and the area around the thumb was purple. I didn't have much movement in the joint. I was getting ready to throw in the towel, pack my bags, and head home. Unless River had a miracle cure.

River opened the door and rubbed sleep from his eyes. "Don't worry, kid, I always look this way before noon. You want coffee?"

"Not a big coffee guy. I'm still growing. Dad says coffee stunts your growth."

"That's an old wives' tale. Just give it a few years. You'll be sipping coffee through an IV. How's the hand?"

I shoved it in River's face. "Not much better. Iced it on and off all night. Did a little this morning. Still not much movement. The thumb is the biggest problem. How am I supposed to hold a controller?"

"In the summer of 1987 I played in the Gaming World Championships in Germany. You might've heard about it."

"Heck, yeah. I know my gaming history. I don't recall

you winning that one. Didn't Lester Morrison win? He never lost a game on Tecmo Bowl."

River tenderly caressed my hand to see the damage. "Yes, you're correct, young man. I didn't win that one. Lester was on his game that day. But there was another reason I didn't win that year. I damaged my hand playing in the pool earlier in the day. I was running on the edge of the pool, chasing a girl, and slipped and fell. Landed on my hand and tore up my thumb."

I held up my non-injured hand. "Wait, you were chasing a girl?"

"I was a catch in the 80s. Not much action since those days. Like the fried foods and beer too much," he said, rubbing his stomach and staring down at the bulge.

"The point is this... despite not winning that tournament I made it to the finals with a damaged hand. My way of saying it ain't over until the fat lady sings."

"Fat Lady? How'd you keep playing? Chinese herbal remedy? I'll do anything."

River gave a half smile. "Close to it. My coach was the great Suzuki Matsui. A Japanese man that trained gamers after a successful career in karate. He moved over to gaming to help with the mental side of the sport."

"Is that why you talk about all the mental stuff? About clearing the mind and humility and such?"

"Yes, young buck. The mental stuff will get you to the winner's circle, if you listen. Back to my story. I hurt my hand and Suzuki applied some ancient Japanese medicine on my wound. He taught me his methods years later. You want to see if it'll work? It might be the only chance you have in staying in the tournament."

"I'm game. Just ensure me it doesn't involve weird rituals or eating squirrel eyeballs."

River chuckled. "Nothing weird like that." River left the living room and disappeared into the bathroom. He came back with a small leather box. River played with the clasp on the front and removed a white handkerchief. He then fished in the box and pulled out a vial of relish-colored lotion.

"Put out your hand."

"What is that stuff? Does it hurt?"

"You will feel a warm sensation once I apply the medicine."

River opened the vial and applied a few dabs on the white handkerchief. He placed the cloth around my hand and gave a gentle squeeze. "This might hurt for a second but give it a minute. Just a little burn. You okay?"

"I think. You know what you're doing? Is this witch doctor stuff?"

"Nothing weird. All natural."

River caressed the cloth around my hand and worked the lotion into my skin. It felt like the Icy Hot I used after basketball games when I had a sore ankle or back.

He raised his hand above the handkerchief and began to mumble something under his breath. He moved his hand in concentric circles. The hand warmed up. "Uh, so, what are you doing? I'm kind of getting weirded out."

"Just relax and let the medicine do its work. Suzuki used the same medicine and tactic on me in 1987. I didn't win, but finished the tournament. If it wasn't for the skills of Morrison in Tecmo Bowl, I would've added another championship to the resume. You just need a chance to play, right?"

I nodded and watched River do his magic. "What if this doesn't work? You have a Plan B?"

"Let's not worry about that right now. Positive energy is what we need right now. No negativity, or it won't work."

I was hesitant in believing in all the ancient Japanese medicine. But I was desperate. My hand was in no shape to play the rest of the tournament and I had to do something. Part of me wasn't opposed to heading home. Yet, I still wanted to prove I could hang with the best gamers in the world. Take home the money and make Dad proud.

"Almost done? How long does it take to work?" I asked.

"One more minute, I'm almost done," River said, pulling back the cloth. He checked the hand and the area around my thumb. He leaned down. "Remember how the thumb was purple all the way around. How about now?"

"Oh, crap. It looks a million times better," I flexed my hand, and it had loosened up considerably. "You're a miracle worker. It's still sore. But I can get my hand on a controller. This is awesome, you did it, crazy man!"

"You can thank Mr. Suzuki. Remember, you're not healed. The hand is still fragile and vulnerable to injury," he said, reaching into a bag next to the bed, "You will need to wear this brace. It will secure the thumb and keep it from moving around. That should be enough to get you through another round of the tourney."

"Another round? I'm going to the end. Will it get me to the end?"

"I like the positive energy. Let's monitor the hand and see how it holds up from here on out. With a little luck, anything is possible."

"Can I ask you a personal question?" I said.

"Shoot, kid. We've known each other for two days, why not?"

"Did you cheat in '93, at the International Gaming Olympics? What I read, it wasn't good."

River closed his black leather case and shook his head. He rose to his feet and refilled his coffee. "They never had enough evidence to convict me. What does that mean to you?"

"What does it mean to you?"

A tear formed in the corner of his eye. "Gaming was everything to me. I grew up without a dad and gaming became a safe place to escape from the pain of growing up. When gaming left my life, it was hard to go on."

"I can relate. Growing up without a mom is tough, too. Gaming has been a good escape."

"Gaming gave me more than I'd ever given it. I had no reason to cheat. I think someone behind the scenes set me up. It ruined my career... and life."

"Why didn't you fight, if you were innocent?"

"I tried, but the damage had been done. It's only until the last few years that they have allowed me back into the gaming circuit. What I'm doing with you and other gamers is rewarding. A way I can give back."

"I can tell you take it seriously. You barely know me and you've done a lot to help me win this thing. You even busted out the Japanese Voodoo magic."

River laughed. "My pleasure. Desperate times call for desperate measures. Even magic potions. I'm sorry if I've been hard on you. I just wish someone would have been more hard on me. When my dad left, not having a male role model was tough. I was a slacker and didn't take my gaming seriously. Or life, for that matter. When I push you, don't take it personally, kid."

"No problem. What opponent is going down today?"

"I thought you didn't want to know your opponents. Wasn't that your new strategy?"

"New strategy... With the banged up hand, I need confidence, if I'm playing someone I've beaten before, it would help my negative thoughts."

"What if they are better than you? Beaten you?"

"Good point. Just tell me."

River checked out his program. "Looks like Jeremy Riddle. You heard of him?"

"Jeremy 'Chubby Cheeks' Riddle. Yeah, I've heard of him. Played him in Halo online. Not a bad player. I'll make quick work of him."

"Humility..."

"Right, I forgot."

"Go back to your room, clean up, get some food, and I'll meet you at the stadium. Maybe hit the hand with ice one more time. Wear the brace, too."

I stood by the door. "Thanks again, River. This is cool. I'm glad you're getting your shot again. The good thing about dreams is, when one dies you just have to find another one. My dad told me that once."

"Thanks, kid."

Before I got halfway down the hall River called out. "Hey, Darius. I'm sorry about what happened last night. I didn't know what to say. But it sucks. I told the Gaming Commission. I don't know if it will help. Keep your head up."

"Thanks, River, means a lot."

CHAPTER 17

If River Wild wanted me to have a clear mind, I had the exact opposite. The dudes that jumped me in the hallway were dancing in my head. The reality of racism and hate still alive and well in our country. I wondered if somebody in the tournament was out to get me. That attack appeared premeditated, as those scum bags smashed my money maker. But who? I'm a nobody on the gaming circuit and one of the youngest in the tournament. Not sure who would want to take me out.

My mind wandered to Dad and the butt whooping I'd get if he ever found out I drove across the country to play in the IGO. He was a strict dad, who meant well. I could only imagine the wrath coming down if he found out. My injured hand was also playing games with my mind. Could I play? If so, how well? Time would tell. Free mind... not even close.

Jeremy "Chubby Cheeks" Riddle was an anomaly. I had beat him in a game of Halo online with not much trouble. But Riddle was a consistent player. He'd made it to the finals in a couple big tournaments and had a nice game.

Why chubby cheeks? Use your imagination. He had cheeks with almost perfect circular symmetry. When he played video games his cheeks often danced in time with his movements on the controller. I hoped his cheeks would impede him winning the next round.

I settled into my gaming desk and glanced over at Mr. Chubby Cheeks. He nodded, and I tried to hold back laughter as one of his cheeks rippled like a stone across water.

The game? Call of Duty: WWII. A first player shooter game set in Nazi Germany, in World War Two. Cool game, but not my favorite to play.

I like the past aberration of COD, but the WWII version wasn't as good. No excuses. First person shooter games are dangerous in high stakes tournaments. One slip up and you get blown away, game over. It gives the lower level players an opportunity to play spazzie on their controllers and accidentally find victories. Doesn't mean you're a bad player, it just means your opponent got lucky.

I placed the headphones on and listened for the announcer to give the signal. "Ladies and Gentlemen. Are you ready to begin the third round? We are down to the final sixteen. The best of the best are rising to the top. And you're in for another gaming treat. Darius Montgomery a newcomer on the gaming circuit, will battle another newcomer on the scene, and a fan favorite: Jeremy 'Chubby Cheeks' Riddle," the crowd roared, and I tried to hold back a laugh, noticing his flabby cheeks.

"Let's battle..." the announcer said. I gripped the controller and checked the hand. My thumb could move with minimal pain. But a tinge of pain would shoot through the hand occasionally. I was praying the ancient Japanese Voodoo would hold up for another round.

The format of COD: WWII is the highest amount of points wins when the clock ends. Twenty minute clock. Unless you die. The catch is, you have other people playing in the game and are on other teams. It adds to the chaos. But it doesn't matter because your points are all that matters. Which keeps it fair.

I strolled down a bombed out and abandoned street and cocked my rifle. From what I remember in my training, before the tournament snipers loved picking soldiers off from rooftops. Major points if you find one and take them out of their post. The ultimate point taker: finding a solider and putting them into a prison. It doesn't happen often but if you can pull it off, likely you're the champ.

Riddle prowled, hiding behind a jeep with flat tires. He popped a couple shots in my direction and missed by a mile. My strategy wasn't to dwell on Riddle because the most points wins. If you worry too much about killing your opponent two things can happen. One, you don't get enough points to advance because you're too concerned with your opponent. Wasting time for a kill. Two, you get killed or captured by someone else because you're worried about taking out your opponent. I liked that Riddle was trying to get a quick kill on me. I would rack up points, lie low, and see what happens. If I got an easy opening for capturing a soldier, I'd go for it. But it was risky.

One of my teammates was nearby. In gameplay, your fellow soldiers carry ammo and grenades and other supplies. You want to stay close to your teammates to fill up as needed. I grabbed a grenade and tossed it into a group of soldiers hiding in a busted up house.

My points shot up on the scoreboard and the crowd cheered.

I had a sense of confidence rise with the noise of the

crowd. But my hand was getting sore. I wasn't paying attention to how fiercely I was moving my thumb around. I had to pay more attention, but it was hard amid battle. My other concern was my life bar. The bar that shows how much power my guy has left. My life bar was hovering around halfway. Not good this early in the game. We were not even at ten minutes of the twenty total.

The crowd cheered.

Riddle made a hit on a group of soldiers and made a huge leap in points. I was ahead by a few points, but Riddle was on my tail.

My soldier crept along the side of a warehouse building. Another soldier on my team handed out more ammo. I had Riddle right where I wanted him. I saw him slide behind another building and had an opening for a kill. A capture wasn't out of the question for the win either.

My life bar was getting low. My hand was sore. I needed to end this before the time ran out. Riddle moved around the building and climbed into a stairwell. Not a good move as the options to get out are limited. I followed him into the building armed with another grenade, pistol, and rifle.

I liked my odds.

I climbed the stairs and lost Riddle. He could be up on the roof or he fell off the building. The second option unlikely. As I turned into an open space on the upper floor, it happened. My mind full of noise, I made the fatal flaw. Riddle was baiting me the entire time. He wanted me to follow him up the stairs and set a trap.

Rookie mistake. I walked right into massive gunfire from him and a bunch of other soldiers. I was alone and had no chance. I got off a couple shots and took out a soldier or two, but it was too late.

Jeremy 'Chubby Cheeks' Riddle outsmarted me. He dropped a grenade in my direction. I didn't die, which would've been better. My leg was wounded and the only choice was prison.

He captured me. Game over.

The crowd went silent and then mumbling and murmuring came over the stadium. I was done. Riddle took me down. Was my mind too cluttered? Did the hand let me down? I don't know, it all was a fog of noise and disappointment.

River walked to the gaming desk as I sat in a daze. I slid off my headphones and stared at the official scoreboard.

"I told you to be careful of overconfidence. That second round match was a trap. Riddle outplayed you. Good news, or bad news?"

"I got outplayed. Thanks, Captain Obvious," I slammed the controller on the desk, "Bad news."

"You lost. It will be hard to win now. You can't lose again and make it to the final. You'll need a lot of points and a lot of luck."

"Good news?"

"You're not dead. Live another day. They changed the rules this year. It used to be single elimination. If you make it to round eight and have enough points, you keep playing."

I let the information sink into my brain.

The good news didn't seem all that good. I wanted to lose and head home. The thrill of the fight was diminishing. I missed home and the aching hand wasn't helping. My confidence was shattered and sleeping in my own bed sounded nice. Even with gun shots blazing outside my window in LA.

River reached for my injured hand. He examined it and

pulled down the brace around the thumb. "How's the hand? Did it hold up in the round?"

"I won't lie. It hurt like heck. I'm usually amped up on adrenaline and feel nothing when I'm playing. But a few times sharp pains shot thorough the thumb. Your Chinese magic was supposed to fix my hand."

River put the brace back on my thumb. "It's not magic. It's only temporary. Can you still go?"

"I don't know. It's sore and I'm not sure it's worth it."

"You're in the final eight. We've come this far. That doesn't sound like you."

"Let's be honest. You don't know me. We met three days ago. I'm not sure this is how you imagined spending your week, coaching a kid with little experience in the biggest gaming tournament in the world. It's obvious we're not a match made in heaven."

"Where's this coming from, Darius? We were making some progress. I never pinned you down as a quitter. You want to throw it all away?"

"Watch it, man. Your resume isn't all that great. If I recall, you're a cheater. No evidence, you say. Anyone can spin a story that helps them sleep at night. I have more fight in my little toe than your entire body. Let's stop pretending we're friends. You're only coaching and mentoring me because the tournament made you. Am I right?"

River held his hands up. "I guess I don't know you. You seemed like an easygoing kid. Everyone has their demons. I know you're frustrated with the loss. But don't take it out on me. I'm trying my best. If we aren't a good fit, you can go it alone the rest of the way. Or stay with me, I don't care. Want to sleep on it?"

I bit my thumbnail and paused for a second. I wanted to go home and not have to deal with River anymore. My thumb was throbbing and, after the loss, my motivation for going on wasn't high. The old school washed up gamer wasn't helping either. Sometimes they say the generations speak past one another. I see how easy that can happen.

"I'll have to think about it."

"Ball's in your court," River said, and vanished into the crowd.

Edgar and Octavius came up, not sure what to say. "Good job, big bro. Lost a close one. Proud of you, though. How's the hand?"

"Hurts."

Edgar slapped my back. "Good news, you're still in the tourney. That should make you happy. Let's keep fighting and win this thing. You still have a shot. Final eight."

I nodded and wasn't in the mood for small talk. "I will need a little alone time. Need to clear my head. I'm thinking about heading home."

"What? Is it the hand?" Octavius asked.

"Yeah, something like that."

Edgar was a good friend. When you know someone so well, there are times it's best just to leave the other person alone. He took Octavius and found some food. I needed to walk alone and see if all of this was still worth my time.

Despite being in the top eight gamers in the world, something was not right. I thought getting what you wanted would feel better than this.

Everyone has their demons, I guess.

CHAPTER 18

When things get stressful, I like to be alone. I did one of those personality tests and I'm a high introvert. Probably why I'm drawn to gaming. It's an isolating experience and creates space for the introverts of the world to recharge. I'd like to see the stat of introverts that are gamers. It's got to be a high number.

I walked to a local diner in Denver called Betty's, wanting to clear my head. I lost a round in the tournament against a beatable opponent. My mind cluttered with external things I couldn't control. The pain of the hand, wondering if Dad was on to our schemes, and something inside still believed the prize money would solve our financial woes. Take down the stress levels of our family life.

But the joys of the tournament were wearing thin and River Wild was getting on my nerves. Did I still want to go on?

A waitress wearing a white dress with blue trim and chewing gum danced to the table. The restaurant was empty, which made sense for the middle of the day. Too late for the lunch crowd and too early for the dinner crowd.

Unless you're like my grandparents, who love the Blue Plate special at Coco's.

"You want to start with something to drink, young man?"

Money was tight, but I needed a pick-me-up. "Coke, please."

"You want a Shirley Temple?"

"I'm not old enough to drink."

The waitress smiled. "No, honey. A Shirley Temple is Ginger Ale, grenadine, and a cherry. It's good. Want to try one? My treat. Your face tells a sad story."

"What story would that be? Is it that obvious?"

"I've worked at this diner for twenty years. A face tells a thousand stories. And your face is saying something."

"Thanks for the free drink. But I'm good for it."

"On the house. Just in case you don't like the Shirley Temple."

"Deal," I said, as the waitress disappeared behind a counter, and came racing back with the drink. She watched me take my first gulp.

"That is dang good. Where have these been all my life? What's it called again? Shirley something."

"Shirley Temple. That's the first smile I've seen on you since you came in the diner. Glad you like it. What can I get for you to eat?"

"Since my day hasn't gone that well. How about some ice cream? My mom always said that when life throws a curveball ice cream covers a multitude of sins. I agree. You have chocolate?"

The waitress stood akimbo. She scratched on her note pad. "Ice cream? Wow, your day hasn't been ideal has it? I eat ice cream when my boyfriends break up with me. Things must be bad. You want to tell me about it?"

"It's dumb. In the grand scheme of the universe my life isn't all that bad. Good friends. Family that loves me. I lost a stupid game."

"I bet it wasn't stupid. It meant something to you, right? That doesn't make it stupid. What game did you lose?"

"A video game tournament. I'm playing in the International Gaming Olympics. You heard of it?"

She smiled. "That's when those gaming nerds come into our restaurant and leave terrible tips. I know you guys..." she said, snapping her gum.

"That's too bad. I can't speak for the other gaming nerds, but I'm a good tipper. My dad taught us well."

"We'll see... You're not the first gamer to come in here all gloom and doom. I've served a lot of ice cream the last couple of days," she said.

"I shouldn't be so sad. Like I said, I have a lot going for me. Friends, family, and I get to play in a tournament I've dreamed about since I was little."

"Little? What are you, like, sixteen?"

"Wow, a good guess. I am."

"Take it down a notch, kid. You've got a lot of life to live. Your dreams change when you get older. When you live a little, your perspective changes on stuff. The things you thought were so important turn out to be stupid later in life. Like, how many middle school and high school friends do you have?"

"A few."

"In ten years you'll barely keep in touch with any of them. Yet we spend all this emotional energy on trying to be cool and popular. If I would've had someone tell me that in high school I wouldn't be a waitress, divorced, and trying to get two kids through college."

"You have two kids? That's awesome."

"Lily and Derek. One is a freshman in a community college nearby, and the other got a scholarship to play soccer in Florida. I actually have one more kid."

"I thought you said two kids?"

"Yeah, one in heaven. Sophia died when she was nine. She had cancer."

"I'm sorry about that. I can relate. My mom died of cancer a couple years ago. Cancer sucks."

"Yeah, it does. I'm sorry for your loss. When I lost Sophia, it put things in perspective. I stopped forcing life into neat little boxes. I let life be what it needs to be. It helps to stop and smell the roses, if you know what I mean?"

"Amen, sister. It's like life goes by so fast and you feel all this pressure to be something, or do something; awesome. When someone dies you kind of take stock in your goals and what makes you happy."

The waitress tapped her pen on the notepad. "That's a wise response for a teenager. I didn't even catch your name."

"Darius. Yours?"

"Linda."

"What? Get out of here. That was my mom's name. You're like an angel or something. My pastor always talks about this strange passage in the Bible about angels showing up unaware. Are you a waitress or an angel?"

"Hang around me long enough and you'll see I'm no angel. Plenty of sins and demons. You obviously have a good head on your shoulders. Perspective most adults wish for. Why are you in here about to cry into a bowl of chocolate ice cream?"

"I have big decisions to make. Not sure what road to take."

"You're living your dreams. What's the problem? Why can't you enjoy it?"

"I can, I do. But it comes in waves. Look at my hand," I said, slipping off the brace, and allowing her to examine the bruised thumb.

"I don't know much about gaming. But that thumb is a problem. You need that checked out."

"I did. My coach put Japanese Voodoo Magic on it. It helped for a little while. But it's getting worse."

"Japanese, what? You need to see a real doctor. It looks broken."

"River Wild learned some ancient Japanese remedies and wanted to try it on me. We were desperate."

"I'd say. So what's the big decision you have to make?"

"Do I keep going? Or go home?"

"Are those the only options? Who's deciding this for you?"

"I guess I'm deciding it for myself."

"Does your hand still work?"

"Good enough. I could muscle through to the end. I think."

The waitress slid into the booth. She tapped her long nails on the sticky table. "I don't think this is about whether you can play. Something else is scaring you. Are you fearful that you might lose?"

"I think every gamer is fearful of losing. We all think about it, time and again. I'm not sure why I want to leave."

"I'm not a therapist or a priest. But I've seen enough people come through here to know what I see. I see a young man who's running from something. Not wanting to face up to things underneath the surface."

"Huh, never thought about it like that. Maybe it's not about my hand, or losing, it's something else?"

"It almost always is. I know it's true for me."

"I just can't seem to understand why, when you go after a dream, it's never as good as it seems. Shouldn't I be more excited about this? Shouldn't I be happy?"

"You just haven't lived long enough. That's life kid. The marriage that was a romantic high turns into the ordinary and mundane years later. The dream job is not a dream when you realize it involves people. And people stink sometimes. Parenting is great until you realize kids can break your heart. Live a few more years and you learn how to see dreams with new lenses. You learn to enjoy the journey and not obsess over the destination. New lenses, kid. Take it down a notch, you'll be fine."

Linda went to the kitchen and brought back my chocolate ice cream. She also refilled my Shirley Temple, which was turning out to be my new favorite drink. "Hope you enjoy your ice cream. And good luck on the tournament. New lenses, kid. Enjoy the ride."

"Thanks, Linda, you've given me a lot to chew on. And thanks for the Shirley Temple recommendation. It's off the chain."

"Off the what?"

"Nothing. Have a good one," I said, finishing up the ice cream, paying my bill, and wandering back down the streets of Denver to the convention center.

I needed new lenses. If only I could figure out exactly what that means for the tournament.

I left a nice tip.

CHAPTER 19

I had about an hour to decide my fate. Do I play the next round of eight, despite the injured thumb? Do I play it out with a slight chance of making the finals because of a loss already? Or, do I find some perspective, some new lenses, like Linda talked about? The dream is still alive, it's just buried deep in the recesses of my heart. I've dreamed of this moment and the chance to play with the best. Am I afraid to lose? Hard to say, but I had to do something, quick.

I ran across the street and dodged a car, making my way back to the convention center. My phone blew up in my pocket. It was River Wild. "Hey, where are you?"

"Heading back to the convention center. What's up?"

"You in or out? How's the hand?"

"About the same. Not sure if I can go. With the hand, a loss, and missing home. This might be the end for me."

"How bad do you want it?"

"Want what?"

"To be a world champ gamer. That's what this is all about. You didn't take a road trip here to mess around. You wanted to win. So, do you want to be the champ, or not?"

It seemed like an obvious answer. It was the reason I'd lied to my father, drove my best friend and brother across the country, and quit my job. Why else would I do such a thing, if I didn't want to win? New Mexico was fun, but not worth having the wrath of Dad haunt me the rest of my teenage years. Or, was Linda right? Was I placing undue pressure on a dream that would be one of many in my short life on earth?

"I lost last round and from what I've heard, Buster is cleaning up. He's dominating the competition. Why keep going when I'm the new guy on the circuit, with half a hand? You still have faith in me?"

There was a long pause on the phone. "Here's the deal. I'm a washed up old guy who had their time in the spotlight and blew it. I could've handled things better when the allegations came out against me. But I burned a lot of bridges and was ostracized from the gaming community. It's God's grace or luck or some higher power intervening on my behalf to have the chance I do. I don't want to waste it. And I wouldn't waste it on a kid who was going through the motions. I saw it in your eyes the first time I met you. You're a hungry kid, but lack confidence. That's normal for most sixteen-year-olds. You just don't have the experience to realize what you've already accomplished. A blemish on the scorecard isn't a death sentence. You're hanging with the best in the world. Don't toss that in the trash."

"Hungry, huh? You saw all that. I guess when you grow up in a hard situation you always lack confidence. You just assume life will always look bleak. When my mom died, our family embraced the likelihood we'd always struggle financially. Was my desire to play in the tournament because I was hungry, or for money? Aren't our motives always a mixture of light and darkness?"

"You're overthinking it, kid. Sometimes you have to take all the mixtures of good motives and bad ones. Let it work itself out. Trust that everything works out as it should. In, or not? You can beat the next opponent. He's had an easy path to the final eight. I believe in you."

Between my conversation with Linda and River, I couldn't give up so easily. I had to keep going in the tourney and see what I could do. Even with a busted up hand. "Let's go!"

River told me to meet him outside the gaming stadium. I found River, he was wearing running pants, a tight tee shirt, and a floppy wide-brimmed hat. He looked like a tourist about to take a cruise. "I knew you wouldn't give up. Heart of a champ."

"I don't know about all that. What did you want to talk to me about?"

River reached into the pocket of his tight running pants. He held up a golden ring.

I raised my hands in surrender. "Sorry, man. I won't be your wife."

"Hilarious. This is serious."

"My bad."

"Your brother told me about the cross from your mom. I want to add to it. This ring is very special to me and want you to have it."

I took the ring and placed it around my necklace, next to the cross. "Where is it from?"

"I never had kids of my own. When my grandfather was dying, he gave me his wedding ring. I wanted to give it to my son when he got married. But that's not happening. I want you to have it. My grandfather fought in WWII. He was always my biggest supporter, even when my life was falling apart. Supportive people in your corner mean the world. Hope it helps."

I'm not going to lie, River Wild was weirding me out. I barely knew the guy, and he was giving me special rings from dead relatives. But I tried to forget about that right now. River meant well and I could use all the support I could get.

"Thanks, man. I can use all the positive vibes I can get. Who we playing?"

"Leslie Van Buren."

"A girl?"

"Yeah. What's wrong with that?"

"Nothing. I just didn't see many in the top of the field."

"Well, the Dutch Dominator is no slouch."

"Dutch what?"

"She's from the Netherlands and a past champ in her country. You need to focus, it doesn't matter if it's a girl, guy, or cyborg. Clear mind, quick fingers."

I nodded and listened for our introductions.

I gave a quick rub on the ring and cross. Any luck would suffice.

CHAPTER 20

I FLEXED MY ACHING HAND AND GLANCED OVER TO THE Dutch girl. She was locked in and didn't acknowledge my existence. These last players in the tournament weren't messing around. The caliber of player on a higher plane.

One of the cool things of the Olympics is you never know what game you're playing ahead of time. They make suggestions for your pre-training, but you never know what games they'll pick out of the hat. So you can't have an unfair advantage of playing games before your match. Most of the time it's a great competitive advantage. But in this case, it was not. My worst game: Fortnite. A first person shooter game where you kill zombies. And this format had a twist. You're teamed up with gamers from past years. Still, my points versus Leslie's points.

I'm not sure why I never liked Fortnite. Probably because I don't play it all that much. It's the hot game right now and I've always been drawn to less mainstream stuff. Old school games are the best. There's a purity and simplicity to them you don't get with the new stuff. Maybe I was born in the wrong generation?

The loud speaker came on. "Ladies and gentlemen, we're off. Let's battle!"

The other part I didn't like about Fortnite was the Battle Royale mode. A hundred people battling at once. It was too chaotic and threw off my game for being strategic and having time to think. I'm a thinker. But that's what we had, no excuses.

The Dutch girl jumped into a boat with three other teammates and headed for another side of the game. They build Fortnite around an end of the world narrative. 98% of the population has vanished. With only a handful of people left on earth, you must fight zombies to survive. I'll admit, it's a cool premise. Sometimes I wished Mr. Morgan, the Biology teacher, would vanish from the planet.

I approached an abandoned gas station riddled with zombies. The DG fired a rocket launcher and blew the zombies to pieces. Serious points. Her point counter went crazy. Not a problem because I was about to take down a grain silo. Hundreds of zombies crawled inside and some climbed the side of the metal structure. I took out my machine gun and mowed down the braces holding up the silo. It fell like a being hit with dynamite. My points climbed back to almost even with the Dutch girl.

100,576 to 100,998.

My character, a girl wearing a tank top and army fatigue cargo pants, snuck up behind a tree. In gameplay it's easy to become vulnerable to open spaces where you can get mowed down by other players or zombies. They can sneak up out of nowhere; finding spots to hide and attack are essential for winning. I took a risk and headed away from the cover of the tree and followed a swarm of ten zombies out in the open. I fired a sea of bullets on the crowd of body eaters as they fell to the ground in a pile of guts and sinews.

I winked at the Dutch girl. She snarled her lip.

For my hatred of Fortnite, I was doing better than expected. But the game was far from over. Anything can happen when you're playing with a team and fighting in wide open spaces, with the uncertainty of what's behind the next corner. One hundred on one hundred teams can get nuts.

The DG rattled off multiple kills as she fired on a horde of zombies running over a hill. Her points cleared the 500,000 mark, and I was behind at 400,000, give or take. I had to be mindful of the clock, and my points.

I wandered off a path into an abandoned warehouse. I climbed a couple flights of stairs above a large pointy structure in a bottom room. A rocket. If I could launch the rocket, I'd make a huge point grab and get closer to taking down the Dutch girl.

The Dutch girl cashed in on more points with another kill. I approached the rocket and tried the ignition. Nothing happened, and a warning said: you need Blue Glo. A weird blue substance is needed for getting the rocket airborne. You needed three canisters of the stuff to get the rocket in flight.

I found one canister on the other side of the building, one more in a bathroom, and another in a closet. I was in business.

The clock was winding down, with less than five minutes remaining. If I could get the rocket up, I'd sail to victory. I applied the Blue Glo to the rocket, and it fired up. I got into the rocket and prayed it would lead to a victory.

The announcer came on the loud speaker, "Less than one minute and we have a close match. Leslie is leading by 100,000 points, but it appears Darius is about to go for a ride. If he successfully takes off and lands the rocket, he'll be the champ."

I glanced to the Dutch girl, who knew what this meant. Her eyes bulged out of her head as she fired like a crazy person, trying to get as many last points as she could before time stopped. I sat on the rocket and hit the controller.

Lift off.

I soared above the wasteland of Fortnite as zombies strolled across the end of the world setting. The crowd erupted and were yelling my name. All the back and forth of whether to stay or go was fading away. I had made the right decision. All the guilt of Dad finding out about the crazy road trip adventure was changing. The needed perspective change Linda preached about was happening. I was guilty of leaving my dad in a tough spot, but life isn't perfect. And the timing of things aren't always ideal. I was right where I needed to be in this moment. Soaring above the earth and, win or lose, it didn't matter. I was hanging with the best gamers in the world.

The rocket took off into flight and I loaded up my rocket launcher. I fired loads of rockets down on the teams below.

I was invincible. No one could touch me in the rocket.

Video games aren't everything in life, but an opportunity to escape and pretend you're someone else. I felt invincible for a few minutes. All the problems of home and life and growing up faded into the world of Fortnite.

I continued to rain down rockets on unsuspecting people below. My points grew higher and higher. The Dutch girl tossed her controller and headphones on the ground and leaned back in her chair in defeat. She knew nothing could beat the rocket, and she was right.

"Thirty seconds. And it looks like we'll have only four

contestants left. Darius Montgomery is about to be in that number as he soars to victory in his rocket."

The crowd chanted my name: "Darius, Darius, Darius..."

I landed the rocket as time on the official clock buzzed dead. Confetti shot into the air and the crowd went wild. I let the confetti fall on my face and enjoyed the moment of victory. I think it was the first time this entire week I was in the moment. Winning and losing was all I'd cared about. But being here, being present, and enjoying the experience was mattering more.

River, Octavius, and Edgar came and gave hugs and high fives. I almost cried and tried to hold back tears. I'd never hear the end of it from Edgar.

"Dude, you beat the Dutch girl. How you feeling?" Edgar asked.

"Good, I think. Everything is a blur," I said, shaking out my hand. "Hand still hurts though."

"You had it," River said.

"Had what?"

"Gamer's high. It's when the world stands still and you forget everything. You're so locked into the moment you see nothing else. Not even an injured hand. The experience all gamers hope they'll have at some point."

I had heard of gamer's high, but don't think I'd ever experienced it. It didn't compare to being in the final four.

I glanced at the main scoreboard. "Final four. Man, I can't believe how good Buster is doing. Nobody will beat that monster."

Octavius, my greatest encouragement despite being naïve and unrealistic, slapped my head. "Yeah, you are. Don't let that giant scare you. You're hanging with the best in the world and you never know what can happen. Keep a positive attitude."

I nodded, yet knew deep in my bones it probably wasn't possible to beat Buster. But I was here and in the moment. Any thread of hope for taking down the champ I would hang on to for dear life.

My phone buzzed.

I stepped away from the guys to take the call.

It was Dad.

And the thread of hope vanished.

I was a goner.

CHAPTER 21

I EXITED THE GAMING STADIUM WITH MY HEAD DOWN, trying to avoid the media attention and screaming fans. Tried to hear Dad on the other line, breaking up. My heart thumped in my chest as I came down from winning the match. I found a quiet area outside the convention center and paced up and down the sidewalk.

What words would suffice? Dad had to know I couldn't keep avoiding him any longer. "Hey, pops. How's it going?"

"Fine. It's been quiet around the apartment. You never got back to me about dinner. Are you trying to avoid me? I'm not cool anymore. Just an old guy. But I still enjoy hanging out with my kids."

"Let's get something straight, you were never cool. No, Dad, you know how it is. School ended, work is busy, and just trying to enjoy the summer. That's all. I have a couple more opening shifts at work and I'll be home. We'll go out, I promise."

"You hear from Octavius of late? He was supposed to go to church camp this week. I haven't heard from him, yet. Usually kids email home to update on the week."

I picked up the pace as I felt the plan unraveling before my eyes. Dad was on to us. Countdown until we're all busted. "He's fine. I'm sure he's having so much fun at camp learning about faith and having fun with friends he probably just forgot to email. I remember when I went a couple years ago. It was a lot of fun and easy to lose track of time."

"Doesn't seem like him. He gets homesick easily. Well, I miss you guys. Don't be a stranger. The new job is going well. Nice to have a little more money coming in. I'm proud of you, son."

"Why's that?"

"For all the shifts you're working at the golf course. The next paycheck will be a good one. Help the family out a lot."

"Yep, so true," I said, feeling my face get hot from all the lies.

I wanted to die. Maybe a car would come and run me over right here in downtown Denver. Or a zombie from Fortnite would stroll down the street and take a giant bite out of my head. The lies were making my armpits sweat as I paced the sidewalk in front of the convention center.

Doors of the stadium opened and thousands of people came rushing out onto the street. The final four would begin the next day and people were free for the rest of the night.

"What's all that noise, son? I hear people laughing and some people shouting. Where are you?"

"Oh, nowhere. Hanging out at Edgar's and playing some games. It's probably the TV. Ok, Dad, well, it was nice catching up. We'll do it again real soon. I'll see you tomorrow."

I hung up the phone and slumped against a wall near the sidewalk. People of all ages from the tournament rushed by and glanced down at my pathetic face. I was a liar and

Dad's sixth sense was in high gear. It's like that parent thing where they lead you on. Pretending they're too old and naïve to know when a kid is up to no good. But they know, oh, they know. And they're waiting for the perfect time to confront you. I had to enjoy the trip to Denver because it might be my last... ever.

A young girl, about twelve, rushed by and back-peddled. "Hey, you're Darius Montgomery. The guy who just beat the Dutch girl."

I nodded, not in a talkative mood. "Yep, that's me."

"Why do you look so sad? You beat one of the best gamers in the world. Turn that frown upside down, Mister."

I drew an imaginary picture of my lips and forced a smile. "You're right, I should be more happy. I'm dealing with some family drama."

The girl pulled a program from her bag. She handed me the program and a Sharpie marker. "We all have family drama. Hope things get better soon. Can I have your auto-graph? I'm one of your biggest fans. It would mean a lot."

I glanced side to side and wondered if Octavius or Edgar had put the girl up to it. I tentatively gripped the pen and program. "You sure you want my autograph? There are many other great gamers here."

"But you're my favorite."

"Who do I make it out to?"

"Shawna."

I wrote:

Dear Shawna,

. . .

Thanks for being my biggest fan. Never stop dreaming.

XOXO
    Darius Montgomery

I always had these ideas that giving an autograph was arrogant. Only famous people with big egos did that. But something felt right. Like it was serving a bigger cause. It obviously meant a lot to this little girl.

I handed back the program and pen. "Thanks for your support, Shawna."

The girl looked at the program and smiled. "Wow, that is the nicest thing ever. I've always wanted to be a gamer like you. And all the boys say I can't because I'm a girl. I will keep dreaming, Darius."

"You go, girl!"

The little girl hopped away and right behind her Octavius and Edgar found me. "Dude, where have you been? The media people for the tournament are looking for you. They need to get a picture for the final four. Everything okay?"

"Life is weird. One minute you're lying your face off to your dad. And then a nice fan comes by and wants an autograph."

Edgar slapped me in the arm. "Dude, your first autograph? Don't let it get to your head. People aren't built for fame."

"Calm down. Some little girl wants an autograph. Says she's an aspiring gamer. I'm not going to shoot her down. I'd hardly call that fame."

Octavius butt in, "Did you talk to Dad?"

"Yes, I did, little bro. Lied my face off, once again. He knows we're here."

"What?" Octavius said.

"Not really. But I had that Dad sense."

"Dad sense?"

"You know. When they know you're lying but they don't call you on it. Do you think he knows I'm lying?"

Octavius waved it off. "No way, we're good."

"Don't be so confident, little squirt. He asked why he had no communication from church camp. You're definitely going to hell."

"Seriously? What did he say?"

"Campers send emails to their folks. He hasn't gotten one, yet. That's all. You're dead meat."

"What did you say?"

"I covered for you. Said something about you having too much fun and just forgot. It doesn't matter. We're all going to suffer from Dad's wrath, anyway."

"Dad's not going to do anything. He's a softie."

"Are you sure? I got grounded for two weeks for being thirty minutes late on curfew. Calm down, little bro. You'll be fine... for now."

"Whatever. Let's just enjoy the ride."

Edgar shoved a phone in my face. "I checked the tournament app. We have problems."

I glanced at the phone. "What am I looking at?"

"The total points of the tournament. You're in the final four. But the only way you can win is to beat your opponent in the finals. Most likely Buster McKenna. He has way too many points, and no losses. A win in the finals is an automatic championship. But if you're going off points, no one has a chance."

"I was afraid of that."

"All you need to do is win tomorrow. And hope and pray you can beat Buster. But not likely."

I slapped Edgar on the arm and gave his phone back. "Thanks for the support, loser. I can beat Buster. You'll see."

"Not if it's anything like your Mortal Kombat fiasco in New Mexico."

"Hey, easy. We won't play MK again. I'm hoping it's one of my favorite games. Then we'll see who the real champ is."

Edgar said, "You know what? We've been so focused on the tournament. Why not do something fun. I heard the Colorado Rockies are playing tonight. Let's get some cheap tickets and watch a game. It's walking distance from the convention center."

We all agreed.

I hoped the game would take my mind off the tournament and my stack of lies. My stomach was already nervous for the next day

CHAPTER 22

We walked to downtown Denver to watch the Colorado Rockies play the LA Dodgers. It was cool to watch our hometown team play in our temporary home. I also appreciated the foot-long bratwurst at the game. Who knew how much food cost at a ball game? No wonder Dad was stressed when we attended Lakers or Kings games. Nine dollars for a hotdog is a rip. But you only live once, right? And the night of fun was a much-needed diversion from the stress of the tournament.

I glanced down the row of seats, watching Octavius and Edgar flicking each other's ears. They were becoming good friends during our adventure. It was fun to see, but also a little weird to have your little bro hanging with your best friend. I guess there are worse people for Octavius to hang with. Edgar was a goof, but would do anything for his friends.

Octavius held up a wad of cash. "Hey, big bro. Tomorrow's a big day for you. We're proud of you and want to celebrate you kicking butt in the IGO. I noticed a batting cage in center field. My treat. We hit some pitches. One catch: most hits pays for sodas on the way home. You in?"

"Wait a minute. I thought you were treating me for being an awesome gamer? Now I could lose money on the deal? How is this fair?"

"Always more fun when something is riding on the game."

"Fine, I'm in."

I could never say no to a bet, especially with my brother. He once bet I wouldn't spit off the top of a building and hit the windshield of a car below. Nailed it, dead center.

I reached across the seats and shook Octavius' hand. "Let's go."

We walked from the left field to center field, where the batting cages were housed. They had built an activity area for kids and families to play during the game. Definitely not something you'd have at an old stadium like Dodger Stadium. Rockies stadium was a lot newer, and it made sense. All the modern amenities sold tickets, too.

Octavius made change with a dude at the counter of the batting cages. I pumped quarters into the machine, adjusted my helmet, and took a couple practice swings. "You ready to go down? I may be a baller in gaming, but my baseball skills are nice, too."

"Stop the jawing. Keep your eye on the ball, Babe Ruth," Octavius said.

I swung and missed the ball. My helmet almost fell off as I stumbled after the monster hack. The truth is, Octavius is the baseball player in the family. He will probably make varsity baseball in the fall. I had no chance. But I could never admit this to my little bro when a bet is at stake.

"Swing batter, batter. Nice miss. Easiest money I've

ever made," Octavius said, taking a couple practice swings, then leaning against the fence of the cage.

The crowd erupted as the Rockies hit a home run in the right field bleachers. "The Dodgers are getting worked. Just like I will work you in the cages," Octavius said.

"I'm just warming up," I said, taking another hack, and hitting a ball in play.

"There you go, D," Edgar said.

"Only two balls left. Better make them count," Octavius said.

I decided batting on the right side of the plate was the wrong play. Switching from the right side to the left was the move. How could it hurt?

I leapt to the other side of the plate before the mechanical arm threw another pitch. I gripped the bat in a left handed stance and made a cut. Crack, another hit.

I had to get at least one more hit or I was buying sodas. No way my brother would not hit at least half the pitches.

In a moment of stupidity, or what River would've called a cluttered mind, I leapt back to the right side of the plate. Despite getting a hit from the left side, it felt awkward. I was right handed, and it came easier to make cuts on the right side.

I must've timed the jump wrong and before I could clear the pitch, it struck me. Not in just any old place. The ball nailed me in my injured hand. I fell to the cement floor of the cages and gripped the hand. The yellow plastic ball trickled back into the retriever. A hole in the center of the cage. My bat slammed to the ground and my helmet slipped off my head.

Octavius ripped the gate open and ran to meet me on the ground. "What were you doing? Practicing your dance moves?"

"Thought I could switch hit. Got cocky and tried to switch back. Ball nailed me in the bad hand. I think it's broken."

"Come on, big bro. Why would you do something so stupid? It's just for a couple sodas."

I tried to stretch my hand, it was throbbing in pain. "You know I can't resist a bet. Help me up..."

Octavius pulled me to my feet and gathered the bat and helmet. He opened the gate and Edgar reached for the hand. "You think it's broken?"

"Don't know. But it hurts like hell."

Edgar pulled back the brace that was supposed to protect my hand from further injury. He examined my hand. "I'm no doctor. But your hand does look gnarly. Does it look worse than before?"

"Still bruised like a bad peach. Not sure. But the throbbing in the hand is like a heart going crazy. That's probably not good."

Octavius started to cry.

"Why you crying? I just got a baseball in the hand and I'm not crying. You're embarrassing us."

"I ruined your dream. If I hadn't suggested we hit balls you wouldn't be out of the tournament. I'm sorry, D."

I wrapped an arm around Octavius. "Shut up, little dude. You did nothing wrong. I'm the one who tried to switch hit. Everyone knows I'm the worst baseball player in the world. I quit after second grade when they started doing real pitching. I was afraid of the ball. Don't beat yourself up. Who says I'm done? We'll give it the night and see how my hand responds. I'm not giving up that easy."

Octavius wiped a tear from his cheek. "Okay, sounds good."

I pointed at the cages. "Your turn. I'm not dying. See if

you can beat two hits. Easy for my baby brother slugger. A bet's a bet."

Octavius hit every pitch except one. I knew he'd wipe me with the floor. He's a stud, but I wasn't going to give him a big head. Humility, right?

The crowd erupted again, and the Rockies won the game. The LA Dodgers lost 11-2. I wondered if this was a sign another LA team was going down real soon.

We'd see in the morning.

CHAPTER 23

I woke the next morning to find the hand swollen like a grapefruit. My fingers were plump, and the hand was sore to the touch. Not good. I called River right away and tried not to wake the guys. It was early, and I had four hours before the first final four match.

River suggested we find a local clinic and get the hand checked out. If I broke it it's game over for sure. He picked me up in front of the convention center in a mid-90s Ford Ranger. "Nice truck. An oldie but a goody. Like you," I said, rubbing the dashboard, "I can relate. I have a 95' Honda."

"Hands off my baby. The Ford Ranger is one of the last great American trucks. Made like nails. Kind of like me. This thing runs like a top."

"I'm sure it does, old man."

"You're in a good mood for potentially having to resign from the finals. How'd you bang up your hand?"

"Stupid kid's stuff. Got nailed in a batting cage."

River shook his head in disgust. "Do you want to be a champ?"

"Most days."

"I know you do. Well, you can't mess around. Need to stay focused on the task at hand. Sorry, bad pun."

"I'm young. There will be more opportunities. I still have to have fun. It can't be all business, all the time. Besides, Octavius bet I couldn't beat him in the cages. No way I'm saying no to that. He's my little bro, he needs to know his place."

"I get it. You're a teenager. But opportunities like these don't grow on trees. You're in the final four of the biggest gaming event in the world. You think it's a lock to get here next year?"

"I don't know. I did it on my first try. That's something, right?"

"Remember that lesson on humility? Keep working at it. Let me ask you this..."

River hit the turn signal on the steering wheel.

"Go for it," I said.

"What do these guys have in common? Charles Barkley, Karl Malone, and Dan Marino?"

"They were pro athletes. Basketball and football, right?"

"Yes, and what else?"

I paused a second and tapped my knee. "Hall of Famers?"

"Good, smarty pants. But what do they all have in common?"

"They all have A's in their names? Come on, tell me, Yoda. I don't enjoy guessing games."

"Every one of these iconic athletes made one championship or finals game. And none of them won a championship. Marino played in a Super Bowl his rookie year and never made it again. My point... these opportunities aren't a given. These guys know from experience, and so do I."

I watched the cars fly by through the window of the

truck. The sun was coming up toward the mountains. It was breathtaking. "Thank you for your enlightenment, Yoda. But what if that was the plan for these dudes' lives? What if this is what's supposed to happen to me? My hand giving out so I could learn a different lesson?"

River slapped his hand on the steering wheel. "Champs don't talk like this. Champions believe they can win every game and make it to the finals every year. You'd be out of your mind if you thought Marino and Barkley and Karl Malone didn't want to win every year. They'd do anything to get a shot at a championship. But it only came around once, and they lost. I'm wasting my time."

"Just like that, huh? I get honest and you can't handle it? I don't always understand how life works and why things happen. But they happen for a reason, often beyond our understanding."

"I should've never agreed to coach at the tournament. It's not your fault. It's mine. My time has passed. I thought we were making progress. I guess not..."

River pulled into the parking lot of the Urgent Care. We walked up the steps to a glass-walled structure. He didn't say much. The automatic doors opened, and we found the lobby. River agreed to pay my medical bills, since cash was running low and I still had to get home. We waited for twenty minutes and the nurse called us back.

The doctor was a slender man with greying hair and silver glasses. "Got a pretty looking hand there. Almost all the colors of the rainbow."

I forced a smile. River sat with his legs crossed and played with his phone. The doctor gently reached for my hand. "Can you bend your fingers for me?" the doctor asked. I winced in pain.

"The good news is you have some movement. Let's get

an X-ray and see what we're looking at. I'm not sure it's broken, but it doesn't look good. How'd you do this?"

"It's a long story. I've hurt it a couple times the last few days. I'm playing in a gaming tournament."

"Video games?"

"Yep. I'm playing in the International Gaming Olympics up the street."

"Tough sport. You must play rough," the doctor said, pulling his glasses down to the edge of his nose. He got up and found his computer bag behind his desk. "You have a familiar face." He shuffled through some papers, "Yep, that's you."

The doctor showed me a copy of Gaming Addict. A picture of me at the regionals was near the back of the magazine. "My grandsons love gaming. They think you're the best. I bought a copy of the magazine to give to them as a gift. They would love an autograph. You up for it?"

I turned back to River, lost in his phone. "Sure. I'll have to use my other hand."

I took the pen and signed my best autograph with my left hand. "Hope they can read it."

The doctor read the autograph. Never stop running down your dreams.

"You a Tom Petty fan?"

"Best rocker of the last thirty years. Always liked the title of Runnin' Down a Dream. Kind of became my life motto."

"You're too young to like Petty."

"Dad got me into them at a young age. Classic Rock is the best. Still like rap too."

"Very cool. I'm a Classic Rock guy, too. Not up on Hip Hop. As you might imagine."

"Cuz you're white?"

"You said it, not me," the doctor said with a smile. "Probably more because I'm old. My grandsons will love the autograph."

"No problem at all. One joy of playing games. You make people happy. Show them what's possible. Gaming doesn't care where you're from or how much money you got. Even a poor kid from the hood of LA can live their dreams."

"That's a solid perspective. Most old people don't see the world that way. Always worried about ourselves. Not how we can help the next generation."

When the words came out of my mouth, I laughed inside. I was preaching a message I didn't embrace. I was the one saying my dream wasn't to win the tournament. Loser speak. I was young and would have other opportunities. Maybe River is right. The opportunities right in front of us are all we have. I can't squander something that might never come my way again. I'm looking at you, Dan Marino.

"You ever read gaming magazines?" I asked the doctor.

The doctor got real quiet, like he was confessing to a murder. "So, here's the deal. I have this Play Station 4 at home. Bought it for my grandsons to play when they came over. I started playing last year and I'm addicted. The magazine title isn't far off. I'm a gaming addict."

"It's fun, right?"

"Yes, and amen. Brought our family together. When I was going through Med School and worked long hours as a new doctor, I neglected my kids. When I became a grandparent, everything changed. I needed to connect with my grandkids and be present in their lives. They loved gaming and so that's what we do. We go fishing too because grandpa loves catching a fat bass. Can't live indoors all the time."

"That's really cool. I'm always amazed how gaming has

that effect with families. My dad and I connect over gaming once in a while. So do my brother and I."

The doctor stood up and checked his watch. "Golly, we have an X-ray to do. Sorry for talking your ear off. My grandkids will love the autograph and will flip knowing I met you. Let's head to the X-ray room, it will only take a minute."

I followed the doctor down the hall and thought about our conversation. If my hand was okay, was I talking myself back into the tournament? I didn't come here to lose and go home. The dream was always to play in the IGO and win. I had more questions than answers and all I could do was see the results of the X-ray and take the next step. Everything happens for a reason, right?

River and I sat in the doctor's office and waited for him to look over the results.

The doctor called us back to his office. He went over the X-rays. "Not broken. But severely bruised and strained. Good news, or bad news?"

I glanced at River. "I've heard this before. Bad first."

"Not broken. But your hand is a mess and extremely fragile. I'm not sure you can play in the tournament."

"Good news? Not sure what that would be."

"I can get you through the next rounds with Duct Tape."

"Duct Tape?"

"It's just an expression. I can make a soft cast that will allow your fingers to work, yet hold the wrist and thumb in place. It won't injure the hand any further, and will allow you to play. After the tournament you must take a break from gaming and let your hand heal, or you'll have long-term problems."

"Serious? I can play?"

"Yep. Let me get my nurse and we'll get you fixed up and out of here."

The sense of relief was palpable. I wanted to play. There was no question. River gave a thumbs up and forced a smile. He could tell I was happy and caught something in my eye. "That's a champion's response. I know you want it. Sometimes you just need others to help you believe it."

The doctor cast me up, and we headed back to the convention center. I had an hour to get used to a cast on my hand. Two wins and I'd take home the championship and the money.

I took the elevator back to my room to catch up with the guys and tell them the good news. I opened the door and locked eyes with an all too familiar face.

Dad.

CHAPTER 24

It was a good run. Sixteen years of life before my dad would take mine. I wondered where did it go wrong? How did the plan fail? Who talked? Edgar. My money was on Octavius cracking under the weight of church camp guilt. Edgar's parents got suspicious. And why, you ask? He hadn't called them all week. Really? Love the guy, but not always living in the same orbit as other humans. You want your parents to get suspicious? Don't check in and see what happens. Rookie mistake.

I placed my bandaged hand behind my back and gave a cheesy grin. "If I had a million dollars, I wouldn't have guessed you'd be standing in our hotel room. How are things, Dad?"

Dad didn't say a word. The silence was worse than speaking. You could cut the awkwardness in the room with a machete.

Dad gave a deep sigh. "I was good until I had to spend my first paycheck on a trip to Denver. How are you?"

Ouch and sting. But not the thick guilt trip I was expecting. I'd already been struggling all week with the money conversation. It was the calmest I'd seen him in a while. "You didn't have to come, Dad. I'm sorry for how this looks."

Dad found a spot on the edge of the bed. "Why didn't you tell me, son? It worried me sick. And your brother lied about church camp. Was this your idea?"

"No, I swear. My plan was to go it alone, and these knuckleheads came along. They tricked me into taking them. Octavius even hid in the car and begged me to come."

"Is that true, Octo-Man?"

He nodded.

"Edgar was giving all these 'you only live once' speeches. He was quite convincing."

Dad turned toward Edgar, who was wearing a hotel bath robe for some reason. "Is that true, Edgar?"

"Yes, sir."

Dad stood up, paced the room, and shook his head and rubbed his temples. A common tell that he was upset and searching for the next words. Not good. "I guess I'm a little confused. You're getting older and I can't keep you under my watch every second of the day. I don't want to. I assumed we had a good enough relationship we could talk about things. Am I scary?"

"You're not scary, pops. I panicked and made some stupid decisions. I quit my job at the course and decided to just go for it. No way a gaming tournament would justify me leaving to Denver for a week. When you found out about the competition and lost your job, it was too late. I had made my mind up. I did this for us."

Dad took a deep breath. "First thing. You quit your job? So you've been lying about all the extra shifts at Swope Park?"

I nodded.

"And you'd come to Denver and play in the tournament, no matter what?"

"Yeah, something like that. I did it for you and the family. I wanted to win the money to pay off the medical bills. I know it weighs heavy on you. Every bit helps, right?"

Dad sat on the edge of the bed with his head in his hands. "Things haven't been the same since Mom died. They never will be. I've been working my tail off to pay those bills. But that's my burden to carry. It's not fair to expect you to help. That's on me. You never have to feel responsible for paying those bills. They'll get paid."

This might've been the first time we'd actually talked about money in the open since Mom died. It wasn't a happy subject and always ended in yelling and more stress in the house. Dad wasn't scary, but his stress often came out on his sleeve in the form of anger. "When you lost your job, all I could dwell on was the money. Winning the tournament would change everything. It's a lot of money. Every bit helps, that's what you always tell us."

"True, but you didn't have to drive across the country with your brother to play the lottery. Did you think you'd just waltz in here and win the tournament? You're a teenager, still trying to figure out girls and real life. From what I understand, this tournament is the biggest in the world."

"Point taken. But that's what teenagers do. We act and think later. You want me to grow up so fast. Always talking about responsibility and working hard and adult stuff. I get that's what parents do. I just want to enjoy the teenage years before having to play an adult. I'm sorry. It's not fair to have this kind of pressure."

I leaned against the dresser in front of the room. I had more pent-up emotions than I'd realized. The problem when the only woman of the family dies is you forget how to share your feelings. My dad and brother weren't great at expressing themselves, and neither was I. What came out of my mouth when arguing with Dad must've been dormant, living somewhere deep inside.

I glanced up at Dad, who was not saying anything and looked tired. "What now?"

"I'm sorry, son."

"Why are you saying sorry? I'm the one that lied and drove across the country. What's the apology for?"

"I love you, son."

"Dad, are you okay? You could use some sleep. Want me to make you a coffee?"

"I love you more than you'll ever know. I can be a hard man, and it doesn't always appear that way."

"Dad... don't be silly. We know you love us. You tell us all the time. You show it, too, by how you sacrifice for us."

"Then know what I'm about to do is in love."

I scratched my head and was clueless where this conversation was headed. Hopefully it didn't involve a spanking. I was too old for that. "Dad, please tell me what's going on?"

The door to the hotel room opened and a police officer came inside. Dad nodded at the buff cop. "Don't hate me for this. It's done in love, son."

The buff cop stood in front of the bed where I now sat. "Darius Montgomery. You're under arrest for the kidnapping of Octavius Montgomery."

Octavius snapped to his feet. "What the hell, Dad? He didn't kidnap me. I came on my own. Stop this!"

Dad hushed Octavius and told him to let the officer do his job.

"Dad? What? Why?" I said, as the cop put on the handcuffs.

I had no words. My dad was having his oldest son arrested. I deserved a punishment, yes. I deserved to be grounded well into my thirties. But getting arrested was a bit much.

The door closed behind me and the cop led me down into the hotel lobby. Other gamers and people staying in the hotel stared at the scene.

I took the walk of shame through the lobby to the waiting police car. The cop lowered my head just like in the movies. Handcuffs hurt the wrists, too.

I guess winning the IGO was only a dream. I was heading to jail. Not how I'd imagined the day turning out.

CHAPTER 25

WHAT DO YOU SAY TO CHAT UP A POLICE OFFICER? Is there any way you could sweet talk him to let you go? A huge misunderstanding, they framed me, call my lawyers. I tried anything and everything.

I leaned forward in the police cruiser. "Mr. Police Officer. I didn't catch your name."

"Reggie," he said, in a blunt tone.

"Reggie... a good name. I have a friend named Reggie. We could be friends."

"No. I don't make friends with criminals."

"Hey, easy Reggie. Innocent until proven guilty, right? I mean, come on. You were a teenager once. We do stupid things. Taking my brother across the country is not kidnapping. Stupid in hindsight, but not a crime. Do I get a lawyer or something?"

"Not my problem. Tell it to a judge."

"Judge? You think it will get that far?"

"Not my problem. Just trying to do my job."

I watched the convention center disappear behind us. The cop took a left and headed down a busy main drag in

Denver. "So here's the deal. My dad having me arrested is not how I pictured the day going. Which will probably cause many scars and numerous counseling sessions. That's neither here nor there. But I have this big video game tournament I'm about to win. The only snag is, I'm in your nice vehicle and heading away from the event. Anyway, if you could swing back around and I could finish up the tournament that would be awesome."

Silence.

"I will take that as a no. If I had money, I'd give you some. I saw someone do that once in a movie and it helped. But I'm driving across the country on little cash. Ok, I'm rambling. I talk a lot when I'm nervous. So, how long have you been a cop?"

"Longer than you've been alive. Please be quiet. You're giving me a headache," the cop said, glaring in the rear-view mirror.

"That's a large gun you got there. Have you ever used it?"

Silence.

He turned left again, and the landscape looked familiar. He pulled the car up against a curb in front of the convention center. I glanced around the car and peered into the streets. "You forget something? Why are we back here?"

"Get out."

"What? Aren't we heading to the police station? I'm not sure how this works. Is there a station in the convention center?"

The officer left the car running, exited the vehicle, and opened the back door. "Get out," he said, with force.

"Yes, Mr. Officer, sir."

The officer yanked out a key from his belt and undid the handcuffs. I rubbed my wrists, like in the movies. I turned and looked up at the massive cop. "Not sure what all this means. Sorry we couldn't have become better friends."

The officer grunted.

I turned back toward the convention center. Dad and the fellas stood on the sidewalk.

Dad had his hands in his jeans and was swaying. He forced an evil grin.

"Anyone like to explain what the heck is going on? I'm driving around Denver waiting to head to death row and now I'm back here. Speak..."

Dad pointed at me. "Gotcha!"

I turned to look at the cop. "Are you a real cop?"

"Yes, sir, young man. A friend of your Dads. He put me up to it. Sorry..."

"Darius, meet Reggie. Reggie, meet Darius," Dad said.

"Yeah, we've met. At least you didn't lie about your name. What is the point of this? Putting me in more counseling?"

"Well, your brother is a bad liar. After Edgar's parents got suspicious, they called me. I said you were supposed to be with him. But before I put two and two together your brother cracked. He called and told me everything. Parents have a sixth sense," Dad said.

We said in unison, "We know."

Edgar and Octavius, the weak links. I should've left them in LA. "So why are you here? You came all the way to Denver to find us?" I asked.

"Needed to get away for a few days. You're not the only one who knows how to have fun."

"Is the police officer your idea of fun?"

"Man, I've pulled some pranks in my day. This one deserves to be in the Hall of Fame. Reggie's a good friend from way back. Works for the Denver Police Department. We had to make the prank look authentic."

"Fun? You call that fun? I thought I was going to jail. You understand the trauma that will cause later in life?"

"Get over it. You kids are so soft. You'll live."

Dad's face turned from a jovial lightness to a serious scowl. "I love you. But I'm still mad. I had to take time off work to be here. Not to mention the money it cost to get out here. Why didn't you just tell the truth?"

"I wanted to. But gaming isn't your thing. And you lost your job. No way you would let me go to Denver. Am I right?"

"Why not ask and find out? What's the worst that could've happened? I said no. Better than lying to your father. The one thing families can't do is lie to one another."

Dad was right. I didn't need an explanation of why my actions were wrong and deceitful. I had been living with that reality for the entire week. I just wanted his support of my dream to play in the IGO.

"So, you would have let me go to Denver if I had asked? Hard to believe."

"Miracles happen."

"Why did you come here? You could've just called and told me you knew. Saved a few bucks. What's this about?"

Dad reached out his hand. He was looking for a fist bump. "You have a tournament to win. I wouldn't miss it for the world. I don't understand the allure of gaming. But I know how much you love it. Good parents support their kids, even when they don't understand things."

I stared at his hand and still thought this was another prank. I hit the knuckles. "You came all this way to watch me in the tournament?" I asked, now tears were bubbling up in the middle of downtown Denver morning traffic.

"Did I stutter? I love you and want to support you. But remember when we get back home you lied and drove across the country. We can chat about that later."

One day when I think back about my teenage years this will be a strong life lesson. How you can still love another person when they've wronged you. Love can be that strong.

River rushed into the middle of the conversation. "I'm sorry to break up the cry fest. But you have a finals match in less than five minutes. If we don't check in, you're disqualified. Can we get moving?"

Dad lit up and was excited about seeing me in action. He wrapped an arm around me and we ran to the gaming stadium. Some kid yelled out, asking if I was in a cop car a few minutes earlier. I yelled back, "It's complicated."

Dad and I pushed our way through the crowds to find the registration table. The girl found my name and checked me in. I felt a tug on my shirt. I looked up and saw Buster McKenna checking in next to me.

He gave me a look over. "Ha, it's the loser. Aren't you the one I destroyed in New Mexico?"

My dad whispered, "Who is that ogre?"

"No one."

"Good luck. But I doubt you'll make the final. I've wrapped this thing up already. If by some dumb luck you find yourself in the finals, I'll try not to go too hard on you. I don't want you to cry in front of your pops."

My Dad raised a fist at Buster. "Excuse me, young man. I don't know who you're talking to, but my son is one of the best gamers in the world. Bring it on."

"Okay, let's do this another time," I said, pushing my dad away from the tables before a fight broke out. "I can fight my own battles. Please go find a seat with my team. I'll see you after the match."

I gave my dad a hug. "You'll never know what this means to me for you to be here. I'm sorry for any pain I've caused you. But I have to go kick some butt now."

"I love you, son."

I'd carry those words into the match. Maybe the rest of my life.

CHAPTER 26

My head was swimming in a sea of confusion. Nothing wrong with Dad supporting my dreams. But did he really come all this way and not have an ounce of anger in him? Seems shady. The cop prank was a nice touch, though. If I didn't clear my mind stepping into the gaming stadium, I was done.

River checked my hand duct taped together with the soft cast. My fingers moved freely, and that's all that mattered. It was sore, but I didn't have time to be sore. I had to win a championship. And I was one win away from being in the finals.

The lights dimmed and techno music thumped through the gaming stadium. Confetti and fire shot out of two cannons on the main stage. Something new for the finals, I guess. The announcer came on the stage.

"Ladies and Gentlemen of the International Gaming Olympics. We have traveled wide and far. We've seen some of the best gaming in the world, and it comes down to four. Four gamers with their dreams of becoming champ still alive. The winners of these next two matches will meet in the finals for all the marbles. The $50,000 cash prize and a one year sponsorship from a gaming company to be named later. Not bad, right?"

The crowd erupted.

"Before the matches begin, I have something special to announce. A special guest connected to the gaming community for many years. One of the most prestigious and decorated gamers of all time. This gaming champ would like to give a word of encouragement to the final gamers. Clement Ivanov, some may know him as Puppey, please come to the stage."

The stadium lost their minds. Anyone following e-sports for the last decade knows about Clement Ivanov. Puppey, the winningest gamer of all time. Made millions of dollars and dominated the circuit for a long time. He was a legend in gaming circles.

Ivanov grabbed the microphone. "Thank you for having me. I've been around the world and been lucky enough to meet some incredible people. I've made lots of money and got paid to do something I love. All good things. But you know what? None of it matters. Playing games is fun and should stay that way. So go out there and do your best. It doesn't matter, win or lose. What matters is you have fun. Okay..."

Everyone cheered.

The announcer took back the microphone and thanked Clement. "Please take your places at your gaming stations. Thank you, Puppey, such good words. Let's have fun. Before we begin, here's the deal. We're playing Overwatch. One of the newer games on the circuit. The format is simple. Last one standing wins. No points. No time. Outlast your opponent and win. Gamers, let's rumble..."

Overwatch, not a good draw. It was a newer game on

the circuit which meant less time to become familiar with the gameplay. Only a handful of people were skilled in the game. My tournament training didn't include much Overwatch and I prayed I wouldn't have to. Well, you only live once, right?

The gameplay in Overwatch is a futuristic super hero style game. You play in teams and try not to get destroyed by the other teams. I drew Donovan Witherton. A dude from London. He was a good player, and I had no experience with him. He was not that much older than me, maybe nineteen.

Our screens lit up, and it was go time. I wiggled my fingers to test my range of motion in the soft cast. Wasn't terrible, but I had no time to worry about that stuff. I glanced up into the stands and saw my dad locked on the stage. He was smiling ear to ear. He looked proud.

Game on.

My character yanked out two long barreled pistols and headed up a hill. A shield popped up and a group of other characters hid behind it. I laid down tons of fire on the shield, trying to weaken its protection. It burst and I made it through the shield and up the hill. I took out a half-dozen men. The challenge of Overwatch is the pace. It's a fast paced first player shooter and the action is so intense it's hard to see what's going on in the gaming view.

Donavan came around a building and fired a few shots at my character. The bullets flew all around and I couldn't see what was going on. It was too fast. He hit me bad and my power bar dropped to half. The good news is they lay power pellets all over the course. I found pellets and bumped my power almost back to full strength.

I switched to a pistol. A pool of water lay in the middle of the city, in the battlefield. I slogged through the water and saw Donavan's teammate to my left. I fired multiple rounds from the pistol and charged the other character.

He went down in a heap.

I glanced at Donavon, who wasn't paying attention to me. He was locked into the game and tapping on the controller like a menace.

The crowd burst into a roar. Something happened on the other side of the stadium. I think one of the computer-led teammates of Donavon was killed. Score for me.

My power was in good shape and I had to end Dono-van. It didn't matter how long it took. Points didn't matter, so the strategy was about survival and luck. I'm not sure I could go for a long time in Overwatch because of the inten-sity. The unfamiliarity of the gameplay was also not in my favor. I had to find Donavan and take him down, quick.

I searched high and low through the little town, which looked like San Diego. Characters and bullets and explo-sions swirled around the game. I blinked and flinched with the chaos surrounding my hunt. The wrappings on my soft case were unraveling. My hand was losing its support and pain didn't help my cause.

In the chaos of the game, my mind wandered off some-where. The noise of the gaming stadium almost entirely ceased. I was a little kid in my mind and running up to my mom as she cooked my favorite dinner: spaghetti. She used to make pasta from scratch. And because it took so long she'd make me an appetizer of garlic bread with sauce to hold us over while we waited.

My mind fast forwarded to early middle school, when the cancer diagnosis came. We were all sitting around the table and listening to Dad explain what the future held. Mom was confident cancer was only a minor setback and the doctors would bring her back to health. I saw in my mind's eye that I wasn't crying. I glanced at Octavius at the table and he was bawling and had his face smashed on the dinner table. Dad was wiping tears, too.

Why was this happening right now? Right in the middle of the biggest game of my life the haunting memory of the past came flooding to the present. I'd come in and out of the current moment with sounds of cheers and yelling and music and bullets crashing into characters and buildings and explosions.

Then it came. The timing was odd, but it was like it needed to come for my good. A small tear came down the side of my face. I wiped it with my bandaged hand. It was like someone or something or Mom was telling me it was okay. Everything will be fine.

I regained my bearings and tried to figure out where I was in the game. A calm and peace came over my body. The first true solace I'd experienced since leaving the driveway in LA. There was a rightness to it. My brother, best friend, Dad, and even weirdo River Wild; were with me. The people I cared about most in the world. It was time to run down the dream.

My character ran down a street into a building with multiple rooms. Donavan attacked a group of fighters behind a door. I blew the door down and switched to a bazooka. I loaded the weapon and tapped the controller with a fierce intensity. Feeling the pain of my injured hand ripple through the cast and my entire body.

The power bar on Donavan danced downward. It kept going down as I landed more bazooka missiles on his guy. One more hit and he would be done.

I tapped the controller one more time. The missile sailed right toward the middle of Donavan's chest. I knew that if it landed, I'd be the winner. Donavan tried one last attempt to raise a shield and keep the missile from ending his life.

It didn't work. The missile obliterated Donavan and the room inside the building.

The crowd erupted and the buzzer sounded.

"I've never seen a more aggressive and gutsy move in all my years announcing tournaments," the announcer yelled over the speakers. "Ladies and Gentlemen, we have one participant in tomorrow's final. Darius Montgomery," he said.

The crowd cheered.

"And a fun fact. Darius will be the youngest gamer to ever play in the finals of the IGO. Not bad for a high school kid from LA. Good luck in tomorrow's final."

I stood from the gaming desk and waved to the crowd. Donavan was shaking his head and slumped in his chair. He got up and gave me a weak dead fish handshake. "Good luck in the finals, man. Nice game."

I stood alone, listening to the celebration all around me. I don't know if the spirit of those passed away can ever be in the same room with the living. But a peace came over me. I think it was Mom. It was like she was saying: *Let it out. You don't have to prove anything.*

My dad and Octavius and River came down from the stands. They were all smiling and didn't say much. We all knew the weight of the moment.

I did it. I made it to the finals.

Now I'd have to figure out how to beat Buster McKenna.

CHAPTER 27

How do you celebrate getting to the finals of the biggest gaming tournament in the world? Well, you get a pizza. As far back as I can remember, any significant birthday or milestone in our family revolved around pizza. We didn't have much money, and a pie went far to feed many mouths. Or it just tasted good? My dad offered to take the crew to a local pizza place in Denver called Mario's. It was supposed to be one of the best in Colorado, according to Yelp.

I'm not going to lie. Things had turned in a direction I wasn't expecting. When Dad showed up, I thought my life was over. He has been so easygoing over the whole thing. I know there will be punishment when I get home, but it's like he's softened. The harsh edge of years of financial worries appeared to be breaking away. I'd never seen Dad take such an interest in my gaming before. He's feeling the joy I have when I play games. I made the finals in the IGO as the youngest finalist ever. Not bad, right? Okay, stay humble. Dad's lack of rage is unexpected. Who knows? All I could do was live in the moment.

Dad ordered some pizzas, and we joked around the busy pizza joint waiting for our pies. Octavius drank Lemonade, I drank Coke Zero, and Dad and Wild ordered a couple beers. I paused a beat to enjoy what I saw. Everyone laughing and telling jokes and having a good time. It had been a minute since the last time we all just enjoyed each other. Life becomes survival. You wake up, go to school, work, do homework, and then do it all over again the next day. Since Mom died, Dad woke up, worked his tail off, made us dinner, repeat; every day for five years. It's hard to slow down long enough to experience life and not just limp through it. Instead of thriving, more surviving.

The pizzas came to the table. A bubbly waitress with a sweet smile shoveled out three large pizzas on our long table. She asked if we needed anything else. The waitress left the table after leaving a few more napkins. She knew things were about to get real.

Dad stood and raised his beer in the air. He wasn't always the most sensitive and talkative guy, but something provoked him. "Family, and our new friend, River. It would be wrong for us to not do something before we eat. To first acknowledge the blessings we all share from our Creator. This food, our family, and friends. All a gift from the Lord above. Second, we have to acknowledge what my son has achieved at the tournament. The youngest competitor in the finals, ever. My son, my oldest boy. I always knew you'd achieve great things," Dad said, raising his beer.

He continued, "Our lives have been hard the last few years. Things out of our control. Tonight we give thanks for all the blessings in front of us. I want to thank my sons for being good kids... for the most part," he said, giving a smile. "And our new friend, River Wild, who has taken my son under his wing. To help him become a champ."

River raised his glass at Dad. "My pleasure."

"I wish my boys would have been honest about their little road trip to Denver. But we can discuss those matters at a later time. Regardless, I'm a proud father and want to share this meal with thanksgiving."

Dad sat down, stumbling a bit getting to his seat. He raised his hand and said he was fine. He took a sip of water and yanked out a slice of pepperoni pizza.

I asked if he was okay. "Yep, just a little tired."

"So, how bad you going to beat Buster tomorrow?" Octavius asked.

"River says to stay humble. But let's just say by a million points."

"Confidence is important, too," River said, stuffing a slice in his mouth.

"So, Dad, tell me about the new job. How's it going?" I asked.

Dad took a bite of pizza. "It's been okay. I'm doing some landscaping work outside, which hasn't been easy on my old body. Some sales, too, which I prefer. I can't complain. God is providing."

I tore into a slice, too. "Good to hear."

Dad leaned back in his chair and sweat was beading up on his forehead. He drank a huge gulp of water, then followed with a swig of beer. His face was turning white.

"Are you okay? You don't look so hot. You want to head back to the hotel?" I asked.

"I'm fine, just need a second. Pizza is a little spicy. Shouldn't have got the spicy pepperoni."

I turned to ask River Wild more advice. "What did you do to prepare for a finals match? Any secrets you can give?"

"No secrets. Every player is different. But what we've learned together is vital. Stay humble and know any match can go a million different directions. Don't force the game, let it come to you. And the most important thing..."

"Give it to me."

"Have fun."

"That's easy," I said, sipping on my Coke.

I turned back to check on Dad. He wobbled and his eyes were fluttering in and out as the whites of his eyes showed. Dad mumbled something, leaned over in his chair, and fell to the floor.

He wasn't breathing.

I leapt to the floor and called his name but there was no response. I yelled for some help and the waitress and the manager came running over. Octavius and River stood over my dad's lifeless body.

I laid next to Dad and pleaded with God to save his life.

CHAPTER 28

THE AMBULANCE RACED THROUGH THE STREETS OF
Denver. Dad was not moving, and they had a mask over his
face to help his breathing. Octavius and I rode in the back of
the vehicle. I said many prayers under my breath and tried
to hold back tears. River would meet us at the hospital.

"Is he going to be okay?" Octavius asked a young paramedic working on Dad. "We will do our best to get him safe
and sound to the hospital. They'll take good care of him."

I grabbed Dad's hand and gave a squeeze. His face
scrunched up and he responded to my touch. My mind
swirled with the thought of losing Dad. I couldn't handle
losing both parents at sixteen. Not sure I would ever be able
to recover from it. I also wondered if this was the end of the
tournament. It didn't matter. Perspective. Dad was priority.

I asked the paramedic a question. "What do you think it
is? He was fine one minute, eating pizza and having a good
time. The next minute he's sweating and keeling over."

"Hard to say, kid. But I would hope for the best. He's
alive and responding, which are good signs. He'll be in and
out of the hospital in no time."

I nodded and felt like that was something medical people say when they know it's worse than it looks. We made it to Denver Regional Hospital. We jumped out of the truck and let the paramedics lift Dad from the ambulance. They wheeled Dad out on a gurney, through the sliding doors of the lobby of the hospital. River was waiting for us and gave us big hugs.

I said to Octavius, "I can't do this, man. I can't lose Dad. He's the only family we got. I don't want to go through this again."

Octavius cried and said nothing. We just hugged and weren't sure what to do.

River said, "Life isn't fair sometimes. The only thing we can do is trust the professionals to take care of your dad. The doctor will come out and give an update on what's going on after some tests. I will get us some drinks from the vending machine."

River left, and we sat in the waiting room and watched CNN scrolling on the TV. My eyes were on the screen but nothing was registering. I thought about Dad, alone in a cold hospital room, and how scared he had to be. I wanted to be by his side. My mind headed for dark places. The places when you imagine your Dad not being around. The images of walking down the aisle with your future bride, or holding your first child, and not having your parents there. Something haunted my mind of the last memories of our time together was me lying to Dad about driving to Denver. I wanted different memories. Happy ones. Where we ate pizza and Dad gave that moving speech and blessing. I wanted him to be proud of me. I always knew he was, but sometimes you wonder.

River brought some Cokes and Doritos from the vending machine and dished them out as we stared at the

TV. A dude near us was puking in a bowl. The red liquid coming out didn't look good. Like blood. "How long does it take? When are the doctors coming out here?" I asked, munching on a chip, trying not to lose my cookies hearing the puking nearby.

"Just be patient. They'll come out soon," River said.

About an hour later a middle aged man came through the double doors behind the lobby. He removed his mask and sat next to me in a waiting room chair. "Are you Michael Montgomery's son?"

I nodded.

"We're glad you brought your dad in when you did. He's sleeping and doing much better. We had to do a minor surgery, but he responded well."

"Surgery? What kind of surgery?"

"We diagnosed your father as having a minor stroke. When a stroke happens, an artery is often blocked and causes an explosion in the brain. We did a minor surgery to remove some blood causing pressure on his brain."

"Pressure on his brain? That doesn't sound good. Is he going to be okay?"

"We don't know the long term affects. But your dad is a fighter, and he's responsive. That's what we want to see. The next couple of days will tell us a lot."

"Can we see him?"

"Yep, come on back," the doctor said, ushering us back through the double doors.

Octavius and I walked down a hallway to a hospital room. The sterile smell, beeping machines, and people screaming in pain were hard to take. My stomach began to flip. It could've been the Doritos but my bet was on the hospital smells. The same smells brought back memories of Mom and visiting her during her cancer treatments.

Dad had a hose in his nose that went into his throat. It helped him swallow. He looked like he had been in a boxing match. He gave a crooked smile. "Hi, boys. Sorry I ruined our night," he said in a raspy tone.

I leaned down and put my head on his chest. "Never say that. You ruined nothing. We're just glad you're alive."

Dad said nothing and tears welled up in his eyes. Octavius came to the other side of the bed and gripped his other hand. "They say you will be okay."

"I'll be fine, sons. I'm just glad we could be together. Not under these circumstances, but I'll take what I can get. Ever since you became teenagers, it feels like we're just passing in the night. I know you have lives to live, but I miss the old days, when we spent our evenings together. When I gave you baths and read you books before tucking you into bed."

"You can give us a bath anytime, Dad," Octavius said.

I punched him in the arm.

"Don't talk like that. We're a family and families stick together. We're not ignoring you, just busy. Being kids and enjoying the time we have before we move out. We'll do better, Dad, I promise."

A deep sense of guilt washed over me. Like somehow I'd made my Dad sick because I had ignored him the last few years. I fought back tears.

"I get it. It's just something parents have to deal with. Watching your kids grow up. You think it will never happen and when it does, you wonder where the time goes. Just yesterday I was giving you baths and tying your shoes."

"Enough with the bath talk," I said.

The doctor stood in the back of the room. He moved toward Dad's bed. "Your father will need to stay a few more days. We have to do more tests and ensure he's healthy enough to leave. We will begin some light therapy to help with his swallowing and walking. It will be an uphill battle from here on out. But I know he'll do great."

"Should I call the tournament and tell them I'm out of the finals?" I asked Dad. "I'm not leaving you."

Dad took a second to respond. "I'm a big boy. You go win that tournament for Dad. I'll be here when you get back."

"No way. The tournament isn't important. Getting you better is the priority. We're your family and families stick together, right? We're not leaving you by yourself."

"Yeah," Octavius said.

"Boys. I've raised two kids. Walked with your mom in the hardest season of our lives. Lost a wife. Lost jobs, and been beaten up by life. I can handle myself. I'm not going to stand between you and your dreams. Go get that trophy."

The doctor said, "Son, your dad will be fine. He's in good hands. If you want to play in your tournament, no problem. We'll keep your friend updated."

I was torn. Everything in me wanted to stay with Dad. The guilt of somehow feeling I had put my dad in the hospital by not being around much of late. But everything else was pulling me toward the tournament. I wanted to beat Buster McKenna. Something in me still thought winning the money would make everything right.

Dad said in a soft tone, "Go get a few hours of sleep. Win that tournament and we'll celebrate later."

"You sure? No pizza this time."

"No pizza... I've never been more sure of anything in my life."

CHAPTER 29

THAT NIGHTS SLEEP WAS ABYSMAL. I LEFT THE hospital around 3 AM and I'm not sure I slept for even an hour. They scheduled the finals for 10 AM. Not in any shocking fashion, my next match would be against one of the best gamers of the last thirty years: Buster McKenna. The one who destroyed me in New Mexico, and the one with the highest point total in IGO history. Who needs sleep, right?

Octavius decided to stay at the hospital. I was alone in my hotel room and had those first moments of silence, which felt like an eternity. My team staying at the hospital with Dad gave me some comfort, knowing he wasn't alone. So I could try to get my head ready for the tournament. I reflected on the week as it passed like a blur. Regardless of what happened in the finals, I got the greatest prize. The gift of spending time with the people you care about the most. Perspective.

Buster putting a smackdown on me in New Mexico, and making a mockery of my gaming ability, wasn't far from the recesses of my mind. River preached that humility is the key to becoming a champ because overconfidence can find you losing a match to a lesser opponent. I was that lesser opponent, and no one in their right mind expected much from the young teen from LA. But I would fight until the end, and see what happened.

A knock sounded at the door. Not this again. I was gun-shy about opening any doors, for fear of being punched in the hand again. "Who is it?" I said in a baritone voice.

"Sheryl Jones. I'm the director of the International Gaming Olympics. I have something for you before the finals match. Can I come in?"

I opened the door and checked down the hallway for thugs. "You're good. Come on in."

She handed me a white plastic bag. It had the IGO logo plastered on the side. Sheryl gave a quick scan around the room. "First, Darius, you have done a tremendous job in the IGO. For a young man, you've shown much poise and maturity."

"Thanks," I said.

She reached into the bag, "A special shirt for the final match. We ask all the finals contestants to wear the shirt. You'll be on ESPN, so it's important that you dress nice."

I almost fell down. "Did you say ESPN? Like, Scott Van Pelt, Monday Night Football, and Sports Center? That ESPN?"

She giggled. "Yes, the biggest sports network in the world. You've done something special, making it to the finals. We want the world to see your accomplishment. Good luck," she said, and left down the hallway.

I took one more glance for thugs hanging out in the hallway. All clear. My stomach did nine backflips thinking about the finals being televised on ESPN. What if I had a pimple on my nose? Kids at school would never let me live that down.

I held up the shirt. It was a black collared shirt with a white IGO logo, and in small print: Darius Montgomery. I stared at my name and a large smile came across my face. How did we get here?

I put on the shirt and found a clean pair of athletic pants. Comfort is King. I pulled up my socks and tightened my Adidas shell-toed sneakers. I might go down to Buster, but at least I'd look good.

My nerves grew with each passing minute. I checked my phone for the time. I had one hour before game-time. One reason for nerves, among many, was the mystery of the final game. No games announced ahead of time. It could be a first player shooter, a sports game, or something else. I didn't have a preference. Only that it was something I was good at, and something I would have a fighting chance of beating Buster at. We would welcome every advantage when playing one of the best in the world.

I stood in front of a wide mirror hanging on the wall in the living space. My cross necklace was dangling over my new shirt. I tucked it inside my shirt and whispered a prayer. Dad and Mom would be proud. I wasn't heading into this tournament alone.

I had about an hour to kill so I visited the coffee shop and ordered a vanilla latte. The usual. My energy level was low from lack of sleep and a caffeine jolt was in order. I'd need all the help I could get to stay focused on beating Buster. I knew adrenaline would help my cause, too. The barista handed me the giant coffee, and I sipped the scalding drink and made my way down to the gaming stadium. Crews of people were rearranging the stage and moving chairs around. The only items on the stage were two gaming desks. One for me, and one for Buster. Every eye would be on the final two gamers. My stomach was doing back flips.

I walked the stage and remembered past matches. The loss, beating the Dutch girl, the Asian accountant, and Donavan. A smile perked up over the steam of my drink. I had sat with the best and beaten them. The screaming fans, autographs, loud music, and glaring lights. My hand duct taped together with casts and Japanese Voo Doo Magic. I smiled, thinking about River and his unorthodox training routines. He was an odd duck but meant well. It was all part of the journey. It all had a meaning and a purpose.

A stage hand with a headset glanced up from wiping down the gaming station. He stood akimbo with a rag dangling from his thick hands. "You Darius Montgomery? Impressive run in the tourney. Ready for the finals?"

I gave the worker a look over. "How'd you know my name?"

"It's on your shirt."

I glanced down. "Oh, yeah. Impressive, huh? That's nice of you to say. But I'm trying to stay humble."

"What?"

"Nothing."

"I'm not the only one who thinks you've been impressive in the tournament. You're becoming an international gaming super star. The youngest player ever in the IGO finals. First African American finalist. Not a bad resume for such a young dude. You must have a supportive team."

"They're not bad. A little quirky, but I wouldn't trade them for the world. What else are people saying?"

"I don't know everything. But social media is buzzing about you. Someone started a fake Darius Montgomery account on Twitter, here..." he said, showing me his phone.

"Wild. I've tried to stay off social media during the tournament. It can be a distraction," I said, handing the phone back.

"I have to get back to work. Good luck, Darius. I know you'll have your work cut out for you. Buster won this thing last year. I still like your chances."

"Thanks, man, that was cool of you to say. I'll do my best."

The man went back to cleaning up the stage. I watched the camera crews from ESPN roll their gear into place. The nerves grew and grew. Don't tell River, but I liked the compliments. Who knew? Darius Montgomery, an international star? *Ok, stay humble,* I said to myself. *Don't get an inflated ego.* River probably still knows best.

I finished my coffee and found a place to sit, high in the bleachers. My view of the stadium, with empty chairs, was a unique vantage point. My only encounter with the stadium was full of noise and distraction. I enjoyed the stillness for a moment.

The waitress in the diner had said I needed to get a new pair of lenses. See the world differently. I was young and nothing could change these facts. But I wanted to take in the moment. No guarantees they would ever come again.

I took a deep breath and scanned the stadium. Imagined it full of screaming fans.

You only live once, right?

I checked the time. Only thirty minutes until game-time. People began to usher into the gaming stadium.

I was surprised when a young kid yelled my name. He came up to me. "Hey, Darius. You remember me? We met in the gas station near Vegas?"

I paused for a second. "Yeah, man. How's it going?"

"Great. I'm having a blast watching you play in the

tournament. You're kicking some major butt. I know you can win the finals," the kid said with a grin.

"I'll do my best."

The kid's parents smiled and called for him to help find their seats. He waved. "See you, Darius. and good luck."

I waved back and enjoyed the interaction with one of my biggest fans.

My phone buzzed with a text. I glanced down, not thinking anything of it.

Octavius: *Dad had an episode. Don't worry he will be fine. See you after the tournament. Good luck!*

Not the news for calming the nerves.

CHAPTER 30

THE ROOM SPUN AND THE FAINT WHISPERS OF PEOPLE in the stands and the announcer doing his introductions were muffled in the backdrop. My dad was in bad shape and I was playing in a stupid gaming tournament. Things weren't adding up in my head. River came to my side and whispered above the loud crowd. "You ready to do this? Clear mind, fast fingers."

I heard the words of the announcer but emotions and tears came pouring from my face, making it hard to comprehend. River asked what was wrong. "Dad, he had an episode. My brother said he's fine but I think I should go see Dad in the hospital. It wouldn't be right to stay. I'll get another shot in the finals someday. Family first."

River knelt down and his eyes pierced through my soul. "Right now is all we got. Your dad will be fine, or he might not be. There's nothing we can do. Our lives are more weak than we want to admit. We think we're in control but our short lives are left to God, fate, or whatever you believe. It would be wrong for you to leave now. You will win this thing and be back to your dad in no time. Just a few more minutes of focus and you're home free."

I watched the seriousness of River's eyes and knew this was just as much about me as it was him. He wanted a second chance as a gamer. But now he had to fill that role in another capacity. He knew these chances didn't come around every day. Remember Dan Marino?

I nodded my head and wiped a tear from my eye. My mind battled between whether to go back to Dad or play the final. I sighed. "What's the game?"

River shrugged. "No one knows. A mystery. The announcer will reveal it soon. But remember, you play better when you don't know."

The announcer spoke. River and I glanced toward the main stage. "Ladies and Gentlemen, the moment we've all been waiting for. Our final competitors of IGO 2018. The last two competitors are standing. Who will win, and who will lose? Regardless of the outcome, we want to give these two, and all the gamers at the tournament, a giant round of applause."

The crowd erupted in clapping and hoots and hollers. Someone said:

"We love you, Darius." I liked that.

"Well, let's get down to it. Our champions have been waiting patiently for this moment. Buster McKenna, hailing from the desert of New Mexico. Last years IGO champion and legend in the gaming circuit. He's dominated the field this week and has the highest point total of any contestant in the tournament's history, without a loss on the card. Welcome, Buster..."

The crowd cheered with a mixture of boos. I liked that, too.

"Buster will have his work cut out for him. His opponent is one of the fan favorites here at IGO. Hailing from the inner city of Los Angeles, the youngest competitor in the tournament, and also a fun historical fact. No African American has ever made the finals in an IGO event. We want to celebrate this historical moment, too. Everyone welcome Darius Montgomery..."

The gaming stadium almost burst with an explosion of cheers. I definitely liked that, too.

"IGO family, one more important detail. The finalists have no knowledge of their final game. We've kept it a secret, making the competition as fair as possible. Our final-ists will need a good pair of sneakers. The final game will be NBA 2K. One of the favorite games on the e-sports circuit."

Ooh's and ahh's came from the crowd.

If any game gave me a shot at taking down Buster McKenna, it was NBA 2K. I'd put thousands of hours on my Play Station playing this game, online and with friends. I was good and knew anything could happen in a basketball game. Luck was surely heading in my direction. I rubbed the necklace one more time.

I had no idea if Buster was competent at the game, but I prayed it was a weakness, if he had any.

"The only format in the game is that the finalists will choose their own teams. They will play six-minute quarters, and the player with the most points at the end of regulation wins. In case of a tie, overtime. Now, finalists choose your teams..."

It was an easy decision. The Los Angeles Clippers. I'd been a fan of my hometown team since my earliest memo-ries. The team wasn't that great in years past but this year's team was solid. Kawhi Leonard, Paul George, and Lou Williams could hang with any team in the league. They were a highly rated team in the game.

I watched Buster choose his team. Since he lived in New Mexico and they didn't have a hometown team, I wondered about his pick. Golden State Warriors.

Of course he did. One of the better teams in the last decade, maybe of all time. Steph Curry, Draymond Green, and Klay Thompson were a fierce trio. But I still liked my chances.

Buster glanced in my direction and gave an evil grin. I'd have my hands full. The more I was around the guy the more I realized we'd never be friends.

"Well, folks. The finalists have selected their teams, and it's time for a jump ball. Let's rumble..."

I stretched my hand a couple times. It was tight and sore but there was no time to dwell on the pain. I said a prayer for Dad and rubbed my cross and the ring on my necklace. Clear mind, quick fingers.

The ball was launched into the air by the referee, music blared through the stadium, and the fans cheered wildly. My heart was thumping in my chest and my palms were sweaty.

The moment I'd thought about since I was little. Time to run down a dream.

CHAPTER 31

I GRABBED THE TIP AND TOSSED A QUICK ALLEY-OOP dunk to Kawhi Leonard. Game on. Buster gave a quick glance and his eyebrows narrowed. He took the inbound pass and didn't waste any time showing his skills. Steph Curry took the inbound pass, dribbled to the corner, and nailed a three.

The stadium went nuts.

We traded baskets and by the middle of the first quarter I'd tied the score, 30-30. Then it happened. A calm and peace rushed over me. Up until this point the tournament has been filled with anxiety, fear, and guilt. I'm not sure why, and I had no objective evidence, but deep in my bones I knew Dad was going to be okay. The tournament is where I needed to be. Win or lose, it didn't matter. New lenses and perspective and being present in the moment. Those were the only things I could control.

I grabbed a long rebound and sprinted down the floor and tossed a pass to Lou Williams. He faked a drive to the hoop. Instead, he took a step back and shot a three in the face of Klay Thompson.

The end of the first quarter and I was up by five, 45-40.

I stood up, stretched my arms and back, then gave Buster a wink. He didn't like that very much and gave a cut throat sign in return. These guys with cannons launched free tee shirts into the crowd, and other memorabilia, while we waited for the second quarter to start.

We battled back-and-forth, trading baskets and eye rolls. Buster hit three consecutive three pointers, and despite the quick points the crowd was now chanting my name and saying: "Defense, defense, defense". The vibe of the crowd had shifted in my direction. I was down by four, 62-58. Thompson, Curry, and Green were hitting every shot, like they did in real life. I didn't have enough defense to stop these all-stars. But my Clippers were holding their own, as well. They could shoot, too. Paul George hit a three and then Leonard dropped one in after a steal.

Tie game. 62-62.

I was in the zone. Remember that stuff River talked about? You just play, react, nothing around you seems to matter. Points going back and forth. No one ever going up by over five points, trading baskets, making steals and blocks, and giving each other nods. I was hanging with arguably the best gamer of all time. No intimidation or overwhelm amid the heights of the moment. Just focus. My mind wasn't focused on winning or losing. Just being there. If I lost I could say I stepped into the stadium with the best. If I won, even better. Not bad for a kid from the hood, right?

Buster was getting frustrated, as I wouldn't go away. Never getting too far ahead of me or behind. He hadn't lost any matches the entire tournament and made quick work of all his opponents. But he hadn't run into Darius Montgomery.

I tossed an alley-oop to Harrell at the buzzer. I was up by six at halftime, 76-70.

Buster slammed his headphones on the gaming desk and was about to kick over his monitor as he restrained himself at the last minute. He gave a nod in my direction as if to say, 'game on punk'.

I stood and gave an arm raise to the crowd, to get them involved. The roar was deafening. This was fun. The moment was everything it was supposed to be. I wasn't arrogant or boastful. I knew how gaming worked and everything could go sideways in the second half. But my mind was clear and my hands were fast. I was locked in and experiencing gamer's high.

The tournament ran an extended halftime show. They brought out an old band called Blink 182 from the 90s. Hard to tell if your career was going well or not, if you're playing halftime shows at gaming tournaments. We were on ESPN, so maybe the latter.

I snuck behind a backstage room to call my brother and see how Dad was doing. Thankfully I hadn't dwelled on pops during the first half. Somehow keeping myself focused.

"How's pops?" I asked.

"Good, man. He's sleeping right now. They think he had a reaction to the medications. His levels are good and they think he'll be okay to leave in a few days. How's the tourney going? You showing Buster some LA toughness?"

"You know it. Kicking butt. Leading by six at half."

"Yeah, you are. We've been watching in Dad's room. The nurses keep yelling at him because he's screaming at the TV. Probably why he's napping now. He can't stop telling the medical staff how proud he is of you. Saying, look at him go, that's my boy, that's my boy."

"Good to hear. Keep sending up prayers and good vibes. I'll need them in the second half. Tell pops hello, and I'll see you guys soon. Hopefully in the winner's circle."

"Yeah, we will," Octavius said, hanging up the phone.

River found me backstage. He shut the door behind him. A serious look came over his face. He knelt down in front of me. He gave a smile. "Darius, I'm not believing what I'm seeing. You're beating the best gamer in the world. You've been unfazed by the moment. Keep it up. How you doing?"

"I'm good. Just trying to be present. Stay humble. It might be the first time all week I've been able to fully enjoy the experience."

"Man, that's a mature response. You must have some good coaches in your life."

"I can confidently say that I do."

"Thanks, man."

"I wasn't talking about you. My dad, a high school coach, Linda..."

"Linda?"

"Yeah, she... I'm just playing. You're the one always preaching humility. Stay in the moment and let the game come to you. I'm doing that. The truth is, gaming is less about your opponent than it is about yourself and managing your expectations and nerves and thoughts. Clear mind, quick fingers, right?"

"That's it. Well, here's the deal. Don't do anything different in the second half. But you're going to need to guard those three point shooters. Curry, Thompson, and Green piled on the threes in the first half. Make sure not to foul. We don't need your best players fouling out or Buster getting a four point play."

I nodded.

"How's the hand?"

"Hanging by a thread. It's sore, but trying not to think about it. Glad this is the last match. The money maker needs a breather."

River slapped my leg. "You'll be fine. Once the adrenaline kicks in from the second half your hand will cooperate. It just needs to warm up again."

"Thanks again for everything, River. I know this was a weird week for all of us. I think you have a future in this coaching/mentoring thing. Even if your methods are weird at times."

"Who doesn't love weird? As long as it gets results. Thanks for being the guinea pig for my coaching debut. It means a lot."

We bumped fists and River left the room and closed the door.

I could hear the music thumping, the second half was about to start. I kissed the cross and rubbed the ring on my necklace.

Let's go become a champ.

CHAPTER 32

I settled into my gaming desk. Buster snarled and gave another cut throat signal. His attempt at intimidation didn't phase me. I'd taken his best shot and led by six points. Stay humble. The announcer came on the speakers, "Ladies and Gentlemen, we're watching history in the making right in front of our eyes. Darius Montgomery is giving the champ all he can handle. Will it be enough to take home the trophy? Time will soon tell. Let's rumble..."

I strapped on my headphones, sighed, and grabbed the controller. Patrick Beverley took out the ball and made a dump pass to Harrell. Quick jam and I got up by eight, 78-70. Not a bad way to start the second half. I needed a quick start because of the three point shots Buster had dumped in with ease.

Before I blinked Buster had already thrown a pass downcourt and Steph Curry had nailed a three, which seemed like it was from half court. How in the heck do you stop the Warriors' threes? I thought to myself.

We exchanged baskets for most of the third quarter. Buster chipped away at the lead as I committed the cardinal sin of basketball. Fouling a player while shooting a three. Not only did he make the three, he got another point on the free throw. Stupid mistake. I only had a two point lead heading into the final minutes of the third quarter, 98-96.

I made a steal and was about to dunk it home when Draymond Green swatted the shot and another Warrior player snatched it up and scored on the other end. Buster tied the score, 98-98, as the quarter ended.

Buster stood up from his desk and pointed at me. He was red in the face and sweat dripped down his sideburns. I gave a half-smile and was confident going into the final six minutes. Not a good place to be this late in the game, I would have liked a bigger lead. Momentum was switching in Buster's direction. But I'd taken all his punches and was still standing all tied.

The fourth quarter began, and I took the ball out. I hit a three, with Paul George to begin the fourth. The crowd lost its mind and the momentum of the room switched back in my favor. I made another steal and slammed it home, with Leonard on the next possession. Five point lead, 103-98.

For most of the game I'd had confidence in my skills and hung with Buster. But something happened midway through the fourth quarter. My mind shifted from confidence to doubt. No longer was I playing to win, I was trying not to lose. My hands got tight and my head was full of negative thoughts. The opposite of a clear mind and quick hands. The moment began to get way too big. Buster was playing with me. Like a lion hiding in the weeds, ready to pounce on a gazelle. He'd been here before, the pressure wasn't too much for the champ. He wasn't used to losing, but he was an experienced gamer. Nothing was going to rattle him. Especially a teenager from LA.

Buster hit a step back three with Thompson. Then

made a steal and hit one with Curry. In no time, Buster was leading by four, 110-106. Only two minutes remained in the game. Two minutes left for the dream.

A pit grew in my stomach. The game slipped away. Every time I hit a three, Buster matched. Every time I made a stop, I couldn't score on the other end. I was going cold. Nothing would go in the basket.

I got within one and Buster hit a dagger three. He was up by four, with one minute left. The crowd chanted my name and then again, chanting: Defense, defense, defense. I made a steal and threw a long pass to Williams. He attempted an easy layup and, out of nowhere, Green swatted the ball toward the seats. Before it sailed out of bounds Curry dove and kept the ball in play. Thompson grabbed the ball and drove it right to the hoop.

With ten seconds remaining, I was down by five. It was too late. I had stood with the champ for three quarters. But you play four quarters to win.

I lost, 120-115. Game over.

Buster was the champ, again.

The dream busted.

CHAPTER 33

I CHASED DOWN A DREAM AND MY LEGS GAVE WAY. I leaned back in the gaming chair and took a minute to let the pressure of the week fade away. The dream didn't entail losing to Buster McKenna, but I had to keep things in perspective. He was the champ and deserving of the win. Man, I had him. Thought I could take him down, but he was just a little bit better today. It happens. You win some, you lose some. But I was in the stadium and I'd held my own.

I stumbled from my chair and moved through the crowd of people surrounding Buster. I wanted to shake his hand; a courteous gesture in the gaming world. It hurt to admit defeat, but he was deserving and won, fair and square.

A large sweaty man trying to get a selfie with Buster bumped into me. He said, "Watch it, kid." I snuck through a crack between people and shook Buster's hand. He glanced down at me from his six-foot-plus frame. "Nice try, loser."

I gave him a puzzled look. Not the response I was expecting. "You don't need to be a jerk about it. I was just going to congratulate you. Good game, Buster," I said, yelling above the crowd.

"Keep your congratulations. You're trash. I beat you down like I did in New Mexico. Next year, please stay home in your trashy city. This event is for the big boys, not little losers."

"Classy..." I mumbled under my breath and turned to find River.

I escaped the crowd and couldn't believe how Buster had responded to my congratulations. I knew he was a jerk, but not on that level. River walked up with a half grin. "I liked the fight, kid. So close. You had him right until the middle of the fourth quarter. Nothing to be mad about. How would you rate the match?"

"Would've liked to have won, I'm not going to lie, but it was a blast. I hung with the best gamer in the world and almost won. What can you say to that, right? Buster McKenna is a huge jerk, though. I tried to congratulate him after the match and he called me a bunch of names."

"Seriously? What did he say?"

"If I'm lying, I'm dying. He called me a loser and a piece of trash. Not worthy to be in the tournament. Told me to go back to my trashy city and I shouldn't play next year. Classy guy, right?"

"Not surprising. From what I've read about Buster, he's definitely no Mother Theresa. He's done this kind of crap before."

"Whatever, it's fine. I don't have time for that junk. Any word from Octavius?"

"Heard from him about ten minutes ago. Dad's doing well and super proud of your match. We're going to get some Buffalo Wild Wings and head to the hospital. We'll celebrate your runner-up finish. You hear anything about the purse?"

"Purse? I don't wear no purses, man."

River smirked. "The prize money. The purse is the pot of money that's divided up, depending on your finish. You should make a big chunk of change."

"Wait, you're saying not only the champ takes home money? I thought the winner gets $50,000 and everyone else gets some extra swag, no cash."

River laughed and couldn't believe what I was saying. "What are you talking about? They changed the rules years back. The top eight now make money. And the top three get a year's sponsorship from a gaming supply company."

"So, how much we talking?"

"Twenty-five thousand. And whatever the sponsor pays."

I slugged River in the arm. "Get out of here!"

"If I'm lying, I'm dying."

"Don't steal my lines. You sound dumb."

"After taxes, not a bad paycheck. You could be well over $50,000. Good work, my friend. I'm sure that'll help the family."

"Yeah, it will. I had no idea about the changes. Man, second place no longer seems that bad."

River and I took a few pictures with fans and waited for the final ceremony. The director of the International Gaming Olympics came to the stage. She tapped on the mic, "Is this thing on? Ladies and Gentlemen, sponsors, coaches, participants, friends, and the IGO family. We have had one of our best tournaments to date. Most players in the tournament, most money in the purse, national televised game on ESPN, and the most fans to watch the action... ever. What a final we've just witnessed."

The crowd cheered.

"You couldn't ask for a better way to end our tournament. A past champion getting a run for his money. The youngest finalist in tournament history almost winning the whole thing. Buster and Darius, job well done," she said, reaching for a medal handed to her by an assistant.

"First runner up, the winner of the twenty-five thousand dollar cash prize, and one year sponsorship, goes to Darius Montgomery."

She placed the medal on my neck and handed me a giant fake check, about four feet long, with $25,000 written in black ink.

I covered my face from the bright lights and balanced the check with the other. I thanked the director and the sponsors and fans for their support. A cameraman snapped a photo, and I forced a cheesy smile. Buster sat on the side of the stage and caught my eye as I exited. He was sitting on a chair, waiting to be called up. He gave a cut throat sign... again.

What's the deal with that guy? Did I say something? Do something? He beat me in two games. What gives?

I ignored the gesture and found a seat off to the side of the stage, next to River. "Buster has some issues. Did his dad not hug him enough? He threatened me again when I walked by. Did you see that?"

"I did. You want me to talk to the gaming commission? That kind of behavior isn't warranted in the gaming community."

"Who cares? Let him deal with his own anger issues. I don't need that noise right now. I will enjoy the second place finish and the cash. Celebrate with the people I love."

The announcer called Buster to the stage. "Ladies and Gentlemen, another first has happened at IGO. Our first ever back-to-back champion. Welcome to the stage your 2018 IGO champion, Buster McKenna."

Everyone rose to their feet and yelled at the tops of their lungs. I tried to imagine myself standing in his shoes next year. But with less hate, of course.

Buster waved to the crowd with a forced grin. He took his $50,000 check and the medal. He thanked the tournament and the sponsors and the fans.

Buster left the stage, and the director came back to center stage.

Before the director spoke into the microphone, she grabbed her ear, as someone was speaking into her ear piece. Her face turned red, and she placed a hand over her mouth. "Ladies and gentlemen, this is another first for the IGO. We have just received word of an unfortunate situation. Buster McKenna will not be our champ for 2018. He has violated our conduct policy. Until further review by IGO rules, the runner-up is now the champ."

The crowd gasped. Then a small rumble of voices wove through the arena. "Darius Montgomery is your 2018 IGO champ."

What? I glanced at River as he showed me his phone. It was a text from the Gaming Commission. They said they'd found evidence that Buster was involved in having me attacked at the hotel. Until further investigation, I was the champ.

Buster raced from the side of the stage and was flailing around and yelling all kinds of cuss words. Things that would make my grandma blush. He was attacking the director and trying to steal back his medal and fake check. Spit was foaming at the corner of his mouth and his team was trying to restrain him. I was standing awkwardly to the side of the stage, not sure what to do. Buster pointed his large paw at me. "Did you do this, loser? Did you say I did something? I will hurt you, and I will hurt you bad."

I raised my hands in surrender and allowed the security guards to take him away. The director waved me up to the stage. "Well, Darius. This is another first at our tournament. Never had this happened before. But I'd like to say on behalf of the IGO and the Gaming Commission, we are sorry that you were hurt during this tournament." I smiled, and raised my injured hand.

"We will not tolerate any of our contestants being put in harm's way. I know this wasn't the way you wanted to win the championship, but you are just as deserving. We can't allow this kind of behavior in our gaming industry. So, Darius, not only is this a first in the negative sense, we also have a positive one. You are the youngest player ever to be crowned champ. And we are so thankful for you being the first ever African American to win the tournament. Two firsts, and we are so proud of you."

I waved to the crowd, took my new medal, and another fake check. This one for $50,000. My mind was spinning over what just took place in the last five minutes. From runner-up to being the champ. I know I didn't win the battle, but I guess, like they say, I won the war.

I'd take it, and knew the extra money was surely welcome. Every bit helps, right?

CHAPTER 34

The Gaming Commission and local police talked with me about getting jumped in the hotel. When I had talked to the police and hotel staff originally, there was not much evidence to find the two thugs. Until someone staying at the hotel told the staff they had captured video on their phone of the incident. Nice of them to watch me get beat up while they shot video. The downside of our digital age.

Later in the week someone spotted Buster hanging around the thugs on the video. The dudes confessed to the whole thing and threw Buster under the bus. The weird part is, why in the world would Buster want to hurt me? He obviously wasn't worried about my skills, as he had dominated me in New Mexico. He was the best player in the world and no one could touch him with a ten-foot pole. Only God knows Buster's motivations.

I took my fake check, medal, and pride of kinda winning the tournament back to the hospital to celebrate with Dad and Octavius. River gave me a ride. He threw the giant check in the extended cab of his truck. "What's swimming in your head? Good to be champ?"

I stared out the window and watched the colors of the sky change and burst with oranges and pink. "It's all a blur. I'm happy about the week. If I'm honest, I never expected to make the finals. I just wanted to be in the ring and see what I could do. Then you get there and you can only think about winning. Crowned the champ after what happened leaves a lot of 'what ifs'... Could I beat Buster, fair and square?"

"Understandable, but you worked hard and did well. Hung with the best in the world. Don't let someone who cheated dampen your victory. A win is a win. When I started gaming, expectations were low. But when you experience some success, it becomes intoxicating. Enjoy the wins, however they come."

"I lost to Buster, fair and square. The title of champ, more like an asterisk."

"Yes and no. Think of it this way. Those dudes busted up your hand. Made you play most of the tournament injured. Who knows what would've happened if you were full strength? The only thing people will remember is Darius Montgomery, champ."

"You always have a good way of seeing different angles about stuff. That's right, I was playing in a limited capacity. But it still would've been cool to have won outright. I'll have to wrestle with my ego."

River glanced back at the fake check in the backseat. "But you're about to have $50,000 dropped in your bank account. That might make you think differently. Right?"

"I definitely need the money. It will change my family for good. I also don't have a job right now. But nothing is as sweet as sitting at that gaming desk and kicking some butt. Winning will always beat out money."

"True, my friend. Probably why I can't seem to leave the game. Once you taste victory you want to see it in all its forms. Even if it's you winning the IGO," River said, slapping my arm.

"It's fine if you have to live through me. But seriously, thanks for all your Yoda Wisdom and helping me get to the finals. I wouldn't have made it this far without you. I don't like to admit it, but I was kind of a jerk when the week began. Full of that ego you talk about."

"No sweat, kid. You're young. Life humbles you. You realize how weak and needy and stupid we really are. Give it time and you'll know what I mean."

We stopped by Buffalo Wild Wings and loaded up on hot wings and nachos. We'd celebrate in Dad's room with one of our favorite takeout places.

Dad watched ESPN and a giant grin covered his face. He pointed at the screen as we walked into the room. "You're on TV, son. Can you believe it? My oldest son, a gaming star."

I glanced at the TV, setting the bags of food on a table. "They're talking about the scandal with Buster." The TV showed a fuzzy video of the dudes jumping me in the hotel, "I remember that night. Almost cost me the tournament. They tried to break my money maker."

"What's the world coming to? Over a gaming tournament? I'm so proud of you, son. You've endured a lot this week."

I took a second to gather my words. I scratched my head. "Dad, can I be honest? I'm not sure why you're being so nice to me. I lied to you, had Octavius lie, and came out here behind your back. I've never seen you so supportive of my gaming. Is everything okay?"

Dad chuckled, reached for the remote to turn off the TV, and took a sip of water. "You were expecting the wrath of Dad, weren't you?"

"Uh, yeah. I've done some stupid things in my short life. But this one surely was going to be at the top. I was preparing for the worst."

"Well, I have a story for you. When I put two and two together and realized your brother was lying through his teeth. And I found a registration receipt for the tournament, I had a hunch you were up to no good. I headed for Denver the next morning."

I nodded, having no idea where this story was headed. "Anyway, I had to stop for gas outside Las Vegas. This small little gas station with an old timer working at the counter changed my perspective."

"Did he ask you inside his house?"

My dad went wide-eyed. "How did you know?"

"I met him, too. Talked a lot about his family and moving back to the area. Family being everything. Yeah, he was a cool guy."

"What are the chances? I guess we both needed to hear the same things. When Mom got sick I was so wrapped up in taking care of her and the bills and the stress that came with it, I neglected my kids. I'm not going to lie. I was hurt that you'd lie and come out here by yourself. But I had a new perspective. You spent these years doing something you loved, and I thought it was a waste of time. That's on me."

"You came to all of that from a talk with a weird gas station worker?"

"I guess so. I was upset driving to Denver and felt betrayed. But when I heard this old guy talk about the importance of family and roots it changed my heart. It was like God sent an angel down to teach me how to see things differently. I'm sorry, kids, for not being present these last couple of years. I've had my head down and not looked up long enough to see right before me these teenagers who are becoming men. I'm sorry..."

Octavius and I were crying and what was supposed to be a celebration turned into a cry fest. River forced a smile and I think a small tear came down his face. He denied it later.

I leaned down next to the bed and kissed Dad's cheek. "You shouldn't be apologizing. I'm the one who lied and should have asked to take the trip. We're not mad at you for taking care of Mom. You did a noble thing. And look how it turned out. My lying got us a $50,000 check. How about that? Mom is probably smiling down from heaven."

We hugged it out and ate our now cold chicken wings. It was one of the happiest days of my life.

CHAPTER 35

DAD STAYED IN THE HOSPITAL ANOTHER FIVE DAYS. They wanted to ensure he could swallow and walk properly before discharging him. And I guess another marker before discharge is passing gas. Dad passed gas with flying colors and we packed up and headed back to LA. I said my good-byes to River Wild and he promised to visit LA before the summer was done. He had another coaching gig with a guy in LA for a local tournament. River said he'd stop by and see our 'hood. River was now part of the family because that's how the Montgomery's roll.

Despite having won the tournament money, Dad wanted to drive home in one day. Save a few bucks. He's still a cheapskate. I said I'd pay for a hotel room but he refused. I drove most of the way from Denver to LA because of doctor's orders. Dad didn't like the arrangement and said I drive like a Formula One racer. Weaving in and out of slower traffic and disobeying the speed limits. I tried to watch it and not give Dad another stroke on the trip home.

It was good to be in the car with the people you love. Our journey was long and the week of gaming was done. I was exhausted but still sailing high with all that had transpired in the week. I had $50,000 in my bank account, and another $50,000 from GameX, a gaming apparel company. They would sponsor me for the year and work around my senior year to get me in some local and national tournaments.

The money was a huge blessing, but it wasn't everything. It couldn't bring Mom back. I was happy to help the family and pay off the remaining medical bills. But everything I needed in life was right here in the car.

The doctors said Dad had to take it easy for another week before working. Doctor Ridgeview described the stroke as "dodging a bullet". I didn't understand it all but was glad to have Dad around. He'd made great progress in his physical therapy and would make a full recovery. Back to work in no time. Which reminded me. I'd probably need to find a job for the summer, too. Dad's punishment for lying and driving to Denver was I had to get a real job for the summer. I couldn't live off my winnings. He wanted me to have real world job experience. I totally understood.

We left Denver early in the morning and made it almost to Las Vegas in the early afternoon. The Honda Civic cruised through the Las Vegas desert air and I saw we were low on gas. Dad told me to pull into a nondescript gas station. I pulled up to a pump and glanced at the small white building. "Hey, I've been here before."

It was the gas station we'd visited on the way out here. Dad left the car and came back after a minute. "What's going on?" I asked.

He woke up Edgar and Octavius. "I want you guys to meet someone."

We did as Dad said. Octavius shrugged his shoulders and Edgar wiped goop from his sleepy eyes. "What are we doing again?"

"I don't know," I said, and tapped Dad on the shoulder as we walked toward the back of the station. "What's going on? You need to take it easy, doctor's orders."

"We won't be long. I want you to meet a friend."

"Now you're friends?"

"Be quiet and just follow me."

We stood at the door of the house, which was more a shack if you ask me. The heavyset man in overalls waved us into the room. The smells were intoxicating. They spread a long table in the center of the kitchen out with BBQ ribs, ham, bread, corn, potatoes, and desserts, lots and lots of desserts.

The old man reached for my head and twisted my Los Angeles Clippers hat. "Your Dad said you might be hungry on your journey. I can't let people go hungry. I heard about the victory in that gaming thing. Congrats, Darius," he said. The man then glanced at Octavius. "This must be Octo-Man. I think he was asleep in the car last time we met."

Octavius reached out a hand. "Who are you?"

"Trick question. I guess we could say family friends now. That's how the Baxter's work. Friends are considered a family."

"Okay," Octavius said, releasing his hand.

The beat up screen door opened behind us as we all chatted. A young girl about four, one about eight, and a kid about my age came dancing into the small house. A man and woman in their late thirties also came inside, with food in hand.

The man in the overalls came over to the family and hugged and kissed each one. You could tell they loved each other a lot. "Montgomery's, meet the Baxter's. This is my family, at least some of them. Remember when I told you family is everything. Well, today is Sunday and we celebrate with food and fun and conversation every week. Perfect time to stop by. Hungry?"

Edgar raised his hand. "Yes, please."

I slapped him in the ribs and told him to be quiet.

The boy about my age gave a nod. "Heard you're a gamer. What do you like to play?"

I gave him a look-over. "Oh, I don't know. To be honest, I like the old school games. Mortal Kombat and Street Fighter. You play?"

Dad said, "Don't be humble. My son just won one of the biggest tournaments in the world."

I gave a half-hearted smile. "It's not a big deal. What do you play?"

"I like Fortnite and Call of Duty. The first player games are fun to play online."

"Cool, I like those, too. Maybe we could play later."

"Right on," the kid said.

The man in the overalls stood at the head of the table. "Well, family and friends, and a new family, it's good to be together. The Lord saw it fit that our lives would cross paths for a time such as this. He's given us another week of life and we should all be thankful."

I gave a quick glance at Dad and almost started to cry, thinking about how he was spared life.

The old man continued, "Nothing is guaranteed in life. All of it is grace. Michael told me about his stroke and we're glad he's still here with us. You'd never know looking at him."

Dad gave a flex of his biceps and a cheesy grin.

"Sometimes you don't know why things happen. But

about a week ago a young man came into my store. We talked and shared some stories. I told him a family and place are one of the most important gifts in all the world. I didn't always get that. It took me a long time to understand these truths."

The son yelled, "Amen," and the room erupted in laughter.

"Anyway, I'm glad we could share this meal together. I'm glad we could meet some new friends and share some time together. Amen. Let's eat."

Most of the adults gathered around the small table and the kids ate in the living room on the couch and on folding chairs. The house was small and not all that clean. But none of that mattered. I often thought about our apartment in the hood and was embarrassed to have people over. Yet here was this family, with not much, sharing food and conversation and love with one another.

Our conversation went late into the afternoon and early evening. Probably later than we wanted to. But it was worth the time. I even played a game or two of Fortnite with Billy, who was the teenager. I beat him, but tried to go easy. I had a reputation to keep, you know. He had some game but no way the IGO champ was going to lose today.

The drive home from Las Vegas to LA was quiet. Dad slept and so did Octavius and Edgar. I reflected on the week and chuckled, thinking about Octavius hiding in the backseat and lying about church camp. It seemed like only yesterday I was lying to pops and heading out in the early morning with Edgar.

Life is funny that way. It moves so fast you hardly have time to enjoy the moments right in front of you. I'd lived a lot of life this week and learned a ton about myself. Hoping senior year I'd learn to appreciate the little gifts right in front of my eyes. Even when it felt like a waste of time.

Oh yeah, I needed to find a job. Maybe Larry at Swope Park Golf Course was hiring.

Most likely not.

THANKS FOR READING!

Hope you enjoyed the book and had a few hours of entertainment to get through another day. It's a privilege to write these stories and hope to write many more.

Could you do me a favor?

(1) Leave an honest review. Reviews are the lifeblood for indie published authors. Your feedback gets more books into the hands of readers. Head over to wherever you purchased this book and tell others what you thought.

(2) Subscribe to the newsletter. I write in a variety of genres and for a variety of audiences. If you want more books like this one, join my VIP list.

(3) Check out another title, and tell others. Like I said, I do write lots of stuff, and if this wasn't your jam, maybe something else will catch your fancy. Word of mouth still works, so share the love, too.

(4) Say hello. I love hearing from readers. Tell me what you loved about the book, tell me about your cat, whatever. Don't be a stranger. hello@ryanjpelton.com

Cheers,

Ryan J. Pelton

THANKS FOR READING!

Hope you enjoyed the book and had a few hours of entertainment to get through another day. It's a privilege to write these stories and hope to write many more.

Could you do me a favor?

(1) Leave an honest review. Reviews are the lifeblood for indie published authors. Your feedback gets more books into the hands of readers. Head over to wherever you purchased this book and tell others what you thought.

(2) Subscribe to the newsletter. I write in a variety of genres and for a variety of audiences. If you want more books like this one, join my VIP list.

(3) Check out another title, and tell others. Like I said, I do write lots of stuff, and if this wasn't your jam, maybe something else will catch your fancy. Word of mouth still works, so share the love, too.

(4) Say hello. I love hearing from readers. Tell me what you loved about the book, tell me about your cat, whatever. Don't be a stranger. hello@ryanjpelton.com

Cheers,

Ryan J. Pelton

ALSO BY RYAN J. PELTON

Adult Mystery/Thriller

Antique Assassin Series

Hired Gun (Book 1)

Stranger Danger (Book 2)

Color Blind (Book 3)

First Blood (Book 4)

L.A. Dreams (Book 5)

Antique Assassin Box Set (Books 1-4)

Stand Alones

The Boardwalk

Watched (novella)

Middle Grade Action Adventure (7-12)

The Ricky Rayburn Chronicles Series

Secrets of the Ambassadors (Book 1)

Mysterious Pirates of the Pacific (Book 2)

Nonfiction

Gospel Driven Leadership

Gospel Centered Productivity

Everyday Evangelism

The Gospel Marinated Soul

The Gospel Marinated Life

40 Days with Jesus

By Way of Reminder

ABOUT THE AUTHOR

Ryan J. Pelton is a genre-nomad author with over eighteen fiction and nonfiction titles to date. He also hosts a popular writing and publishing podcast, The Prolific Writer. Ryan reads, writes, naps, and nurses a Diet Coke addiction, with his wife and four children in Kansas City, Missouri. Find Ryan and his work at: ryanjpelton.com